THE WRONG BROTHER

LOVE YOU FOREVER-BOOK 1

ALEXIS WINTER

ROCK BOTTOM HAS A BASEMENT—
AND I JUST FOUND IT.

I've been head over heels, write it in my diary over and over in love with my best friend Preston Young, pretty much my entire life.

You'd think after decades of hiding my feelings I'd want to reveal my lifelong secret love to my best friend privately, but NOPE.
As the queen of ridiculously grand romantic gestures,
I chose a Jerry Springer style television reveal.

I'll spare you the anxiety inducing details and just say, it didn't...*work out* the way I thought it would.
Cue crawling into a deep dark hole of wine, ice cream and sad ass movies.
I'm never showing my face again.

Okay, so maybe he stormed off the stage and rejected me on live television.
And maybe when his older brother came over to comfort me...I kissed him.

So much for getting my sh*t together.

It was just a kiss.
And then a few more.
And then so many toe-curling O's my brains are permanently
scrambled.

One minute I'm pining for my best friend,
The next I'm falling for his brother,
And to make matters worse...now my best friend thinks he might be
in love with me?
I didn't know it was even possible to screw up this bad.

**Am I destined to make one giant laughable mistake out
of my life,
Or did I miss what's been right in front of me this
entire time?**

ONE

PIPER

The text from Preston, my best friend and secret crush, reads: *What time will you be home tonight?*

I roll my eyes as I quickly respond *should be there by 8 p.m.* I've told him this time and time again since mentioning it last week.

Eight? Why so late?

I shake my head and I can't help but laugh to myself, wondering if he's been drunk every time we've talked but knowing...that's just Preston. "Does he ever actually listen when I talk?" I say to myself as I type out my response. *I don't get off work until 5 p.m., then I have to make the drive.*

Late dinner and drinks?

You know it. I drop the phone onto the bed by my side and look at the clock on the bedside table. It's going on 7 a.m. My alarm will be going off in the next two minutes. I push the blankets back and turn off the alarm since I'm already up. There's nothing worse than hearing that loud blaring sound first thing in the morning. I stand from bed and push my oversized T-shirt back down my thighs before stretching and starting for the kitchen.

I start a pot of coffee and stand by the counter impatiently as it brews. As I wait, I look over the white subway tile backsplash, the gray granite countertops, and the crisp white cabinets with shiny silver knobs. I've only recently renovated my kitchen and I'm absolutely in love with it.

I bought this old rundown townhouse with the intention of bringing it back to life. At the low price point, I couldn't turn it down. Plus, it's the perfect size for the family I plan to have one day. There are three bedrooms, two bathrooms, an eat-in kitchen, a living room, plus a laundry room. Most of the rooms aren't being used right now, but that just gives me more time to get everything exactly how I want it. Now that the kitchen is finished, the bedrooms will be my main focus.

I saved a ton by buying this house in the condition it was in, and I'm saving even more doing most of the work myself. The work I can't do, my dad can help me with, only hiring out if the job is too big for them both. So far, the only thing I've hired out has been the new brick and vinyl siding on the house, and the landscaping. This house may have been trashed when I bought it, but the homeowners' association is expecting it to look just like the rest of the homes in our gated community. I can take as long as I want to do the inside, but the outside had to be the first priority.

The coffee finally finishes brewing and I waste no time pouring a cup to take to the bathroom with me. I take a sip before washing my face and lathering on my $80 moisturizer. I put on my usual makeup and get busy curling my honey-blonde hair. I finish my cup of coffee and brush my teeth before going to get dressed. I pull on a pair of gray dress pants and a ruffly white top. I gather everything I'll need for the day and pour more coffee into a to-go cup before walking out to the garage.

I toss my purse and computer bag into the passenger-side seat and start up my silver Honda Civic. I click the button and the garage door rolls upward. I back out and hit the button again to close it as I drive off. I'm stuck on the freeway in morning traffic when my stereo tells me I have another text from Preston.

Danny is going to join us for dinner. Anything specific you want? I'll make reservations.

I snort. Preston make reservations? In Middleton? I didn't even know there were any restaurants that *took* reservations.

Let's go for pizza and beer at Tino's. Keep it casual.

As I wait for traffic to move again, I imagine telling Preston my deepest, darkest secret. I can see the stunned expression on his face: dark brows drawing together, icy eyes glazing over as he processes the information I've given him, running his hand through his messy-but-styled dark hair. He opens his mouth to respond, but the car behind me honks its horn, pulling me from my fantasy.

"All right, all right. I'm going," I mumble to myself as I hit the gas.

It's funny, because I've imagined telling Preston how I really feel many times over the years, however, I never seem to figure out what he would say. Would he get angry? Would be confess his own attraction? I don't know. And that's exactly why I've never uttered those words to him.

Preston and I, along with his older brother, Calvin, grew up together. It didn't hurt that his house was right across the street and our parents have been the best of friends for as long as I can remember. Preston and I were always together. While Calvin is clearly the better choice if someone's looking for a relationship, Preston is the one my body has always craved.

Well, I shouldn't say *always*. We were like best friends when we were little, then that *boys have cooties* phase kicked in. Even though I was deathly afraid of catching his cooties, we still made sure to cause trouble where we could. Preston was always the attention-seeker of the two brothers. It's like he was addicted to it. If too much time had passed with him going unnoticed, he'd make sure to get the attention of everyone in his vicinity.

If I had to pinpoint the exact moment Preston stole my attention for a whole different reason, I'd say it was the summer between freshman and sophomore year. He'd been away with his traveling baseball team.

I remember Calvin and I were hanging out in his backyard, chilling by the pool, when Preston arrived home. He walked out the patio door, looked over at his brother, then met my eyes. He smirked and the sun was shining down on his dark hair that had natural highlights from spending the summer on the field. With his icy gaze on mine, he pulled off his shirt, revealing a rock-hard chest and defined abs. Over the summer, he'd changed from a teenage boy to a man, and I was in love. In those two seconds, I imagined pushing him up against the wooden privacy fence in his backyard and taking what I never knew I wanted until that moment. I saw us falling in love, getting married, having children, and kissing every second of every day. Then he jumped into the pool and the cold water splashed me, pulling me out of my daydream.

Since that day so many years ago, Preston has only managed to get better-looking. His body has become even more manly—so defined and hard. His angular jaw has become sharper, and he now has dark stubble across it that I imagine would feel amazing against my skin. His blue eyes are still icy, but they now hold knowledge and secrets, making them even more enthralling. His skin is always tanned from being in the sun—he loves anything outdoors—and his dark hair has somehow managed to keep those natural highlights that are a mix of caramel and cinnamon. The man belongs in an Abercrombie catalog.

With a face and a body like his, he gets everything he wants, and that means *everything*—including women. Any woman would be proud to have him on her arm. Hell, any woman would brag about a one-night stand with him. There would be no shame in confessing you had a short-lived fling with this man. In fact, I think there's a local club for said women. *Raise your hand if you're another notch on Preston Young's bedpost.*

I know you're probably wondering: *Are you another notch on the bedpost?* Well, my friend, I must admit I am not. Sadly. While Preston is what you could call a womanizer, he's always held his relationship with me to a higher level. The most we've ever done is a drunken kiss during a game of spin the bottle back in high school. And let me tell you, it was what dreams are made of. But deep down, I wonder if Preston even sees me as a woman. For years I've wondered: *What's wrong with me? Why doesn't he ever flirt with me? Why doesn't he want to have a drunken one-night stand with me?* The answers to those questions are still unanswered because I'm too afraid to ask them out loud.

I finally manage to make it to the *Wonder Home Magazine* office. *Wonder Home Magazine* is fairly new to the shelves when you compare it with other publications in the same genre, like *Better Homes & Gardens*. Our main focus is giving ideas and inspiration to transform an old, outdated home into something more beautiful and modern while still holding on to its classic charm.

I have to admit, the things I've learned by writing here have been put into action during my current home remodel. I can't wait to learn more and apply it to my own place. I've only worked here a year, so I'm still fairly new and get assigned the smaller articles. It's my dream to work my way to the top, writing the hard-hitting features that make the front cover—maybe even moving up to become editor-in-chief.

I drop off my things at my desk before heading to the break room to load up on the sugar I'll need to finish my article and get out of here. I grab two glazed donuts and take them back to my desk. Turning on the computer, I take a bite and wash it down with my coffee. By the time my computer is up and running, and I've returned all the necessary emails, my sugar-and-caffeine buzz has kicked in enough to get to work.

I write a meaningless article on how to turn pallets into garden and patio additions—swings, planters, patio furniture, and fire pits—then read it over before submitting the story for approval. While I wait to hear back, I grab my phone and call my mom to make sure she remembers I'm coming home tonight.

"Hey, honey," she answers.

I smile from her always-sweet and welcoming tone. "Hey, Mom. What's up?"

"Oh, you know, just working in the flower beds while watching your dad try to build me that built-in grill you wrote about."

I laugh. "Are you serious? You got Daddy to build you that grill?"

"Well, it was lovely and I think it would look great out on the patio, don't you?"

"Well, yeah, but . . ."

"No buts. What I want, I get," she giggles out.

"Whatever you say. You guys remember I'm coming home tonight, right?"

"Of course, dear. Your room is already made up with fresh bedding."

"Mom, you didn't have to change the bedding."

"I really did. Your Uncle Peter and Aunt Beth stayed with us last weekend. Between you and me, I think something freaky went down in that bed. Maybe I should buy a new one."

My mouth drops open and I can't hold back my laugh. "Gross! Why would you tell me that?"

She laughs. "You know how much I love messing with your head."

"I'll probably have nightmares now, Mother."

This only makes her laugh harder. "Well, they did forget a book on the nightstand. It was *Kama*-something . . . *Kama Sutra* maybe?"

"Ugh," I groan. "Mom, stop talking."

She laughs. "I'll see you this evening."

"Bye, Mom." I hang up the phone and shiver with disgust.

To give you the mental picture I have, imagine this: My Uncle Peter, who is my dad's brother, is about 250 pounds. He's short and round and covered in patches of dark curly hair—everywhere but the top of his head, that is. His wife, my Aunt Beth, is tall like an Amazon. She easily towers over my uncle. She's built like a linebacker. I mean, they've been married for years, so of course they have sex, but that's not what I want to picture when I climb into my childhood bed.

Another shiver runs through me, but I shake it off when I see an email pop into my inbox with the subject line "Article Approved." With a smile on my face, I sign out and pack my things. I'm happy I get to leave early. This will give me more time to spend at home with Preston and my family. It's going on 2 p.m. when I make it to the parking lot, and it's nearly 3 p.m. by the time I'm packing my car for the weekend.

As I make the long drive home to central Illinois, my mind goes back to the daydream I always have, only this time, when I tell Preston how I feel, he looks at me with pity as he shares the news of his recent engagement. That *would* be my luck. You'd think that since these are my daydreams, I'd have control over them, but nope. They surprise me just as much as they would anyone else. Things like this make me not want to tell him how I feel at all.

Instead of thinking about what his reaction might be, I instead try to remember the good times we've shared. Like that drunken kiss when I was 16.

I reach out and spin the bottle. Everyone watches intently as it spins and spins. I look away, glancing at all the smiling guys who are watching the bottle spin. And then I look at the one guy I want to kiss. He isn't smiling. In fact, he looks a little afraid that it'll land on him.

The bottle starts to slow and I watch it, willing it to land on Preston. Like I had some kind of mental control over it, the bottle stops and I follow the neck to see where it's pointing. Preston.

His eyes are wide with fear and his lips are slightly parted. I smile up at him as his tongue slips out, wetting his lips. Everyone in the circle is hooting and cheering, clapping and whispering. So many of them have questioned our relationship before. I mean, Preston sleeps with everyone and I'm already around him all the time anyway. They can't figure out if we've slept together or if we're really just the friends we claim to be.

I get up on my knees and lean toward the center of the circle as Preston does the same, only he doesn't shy away. He doesn't move slowly like I'm doing. He's in a hurry—whether it's a hurry to kiss me or a hurry to get it over with, I don't know, but he doesn't waste any time.

He reaches for me and his hand lands on the base of my neck, pulling my lips to his. His lips are soft and strong—sweet but with the lingering bitterness of beer. His tongue rubs against mine and my eyes flutter closed. My entire body feels like it's been lit on fire. I don't know if it's the embarrassment I feel with everyone watching or if it's because he's touching me, but it's a burn I enjoy nonetheless.

Just as I place my arms around his neck, he pulls away. His face is red and his eyes are glassy. His body seems harder than it did before and his back is straight. I smile as a giggle escapes at the awkwardness of our moment, but he's stock-still, not smiling, not moving, not even looking at me.

The kiss itself was amazing, but the way he acted like he'd just been made to eat a worm was a bit of a turnoff. I still can't figure out why. Was he repulsed by the thought of kissing me? Was it all a show to make everyone believe kissing wasn't something we'd done before? Was he worried it'd end our friendship?

I guess I'll never really know, because I'll never get up the nerve to ask him. I can live with not knowing; I've done it this long. What I can't live with is his rejection—not after I've seen him with the quantity of women I have. He's never turned down anyone. It's only ever been me, so I prefer to believe it's because we're friends and he doesn't want to risk what we have. Yes, that sounds better than the thought that I'm not good enough.

TWO
PIPER

I turn onto my old street and already my childhood home is in clear view. The blue two-story house with black shutters, a two-car garage, and perfectly-planted flowers look just as they always have. I pull into the driveway and park the car. Mom is down on her hands and knees, weeding the flowers that line the foundation of the house. She turns and looks over at me with a wide smile.

She squeals as she stands up, running over to me as I'm exiting the car. Her honey-blonde hair that matches mine is bouncing as she runs. She wraps me in a big hug and squeezes the life out of me. "It's so good to have you home."

I hug her tightly and inhale her familiar scent that always seems to calm me down. "Let's go see how you've been torturing Dad," I joke as she pulls away with a snicker.

I grab my bag and follow her around the house and through the gate in the privacy fence. Dad is standing in the back half of the yard, beside the pool house on the other side of the in-ground pool. And he's surrounded by a massive pile of bricks.

He's stripped off his shirt and his beer belly is hanging over his basketball shorts. His back and shoulders are red and sunburned from spending the day working on Mom's built-in grill. He hasn't noticed us yet.

"Damn that fucking magazine," he grumbles as he picks up another brick. "Why in the hell did I even get married to begin with? Someone should've told me I'd be doing this shit. I would've backed out for sure."

"Yeah, but then you wouldn't have had me," I say, pulling him from his ramblings.

He turns to look over at Mom and me. She's standing beside me with her hands on her hips, shooting daggers at him with her eyes.

He puts on a fake smile. "I was just teasing. You know I don't mean a word of it," he tells Mom, giving her his best flirty smile.

"Mm-hmm, I know. If it wasn't for me, you'd probably be dead already," she says as we walk over.

Dad leans in and gives me a hug. "Cancel our subscription to the magazine please," he whispers low enough so she won't hear.

I laugh. "You know I can't do that. She'd figure it out and resubscribe at full price, or download it to her iPad and read it in the bathroom."

He lets out a sigh as he pulls away. He gives Mom the best puppy-dog eyes he can muster.

I look at the grill. "Well, it looks like it's coming along nicely. You're doing a good job, Dad."

He laughs. "Yeah, but with my luck, this won't be anything but a decoration. It has to be sealed perfectly to cook right."

"I'm sure you'll manage. You're good at building stuff like this."

"He really is. Next, I want to do the outdoor fireplace and seating area like what was on the cover of last month's magazine. I'm thinking right over there," Mom says, pointing to the opposite side of the yard.

Dad growls and returns to his work.

She giggles as she takes my hand and pulls me toward the house.

"What's gotten you on the home-improvement kick, Mom?" I ask as I sit at the island in the kitchen, watching as she pulls out a pitcher of lemonade from the fridge and pours three glasses.

"He's retired, so he needs something to keep him busy. Plus, imagine the parties we could have out there. We have the nice pool and the pool house for any guests who need a place to crash. The pool house has a bar. We could have a cookout followed by a pool party, then end it with a dip in the hot tub with the fire crackling next to it."

"Hot tub? Does Dad know about that one?"

She giggles. "Not yet. One thing at a time, dear."

I laugh and shake my head.

"You have plans with Preston tonight?"

I frown. "Why would you think that?" No one knows about my crush on Preston—not even my own mother. Well, I confided in Calvin back in the day, but I'm sure he assumes it was just a high school thing. I'm sure he doesn't think I'm pathetic enough to pine for someone for over a decade.

She shrugs. "You usually do, don't you? When you're both in town at the same time, you usually get together for dinner."

I nod. "Yeah, we're going for pizza and beer."

She shoots me a look. "Better make sure your father doesn't get a call at 3 a.m. to come bail the two of you out of jail."

"That was *one* time, Mom."

"No, it was only one time when it happened at 3 a.m. I believe we've had to bail the two of you out at least four times, and his parents have had their fair share too."

I smile, knowing it's completely true. We took turns on whose parents we'd call. And we never did anything truly bad. It was all for stupid stuff like breaking curfew, and breaking and entering on the closed high school football field. We weren't going to destroy it—we just wanted to hang on the 50-yard line while polishing off a bottle of vodka Preston stole from his dad.

Though one time we did get arrested for starting a bar fight. I'd been dating this jerk and Preston found out he was cheating on me. When he showed up, they got into a fight. The girl he was cheating on me with jumped on Preston to peel him off said jerk, and I couldn't let that slide. I jumped on her, ending the fight because Preston and Jerkface couldn't do anything with two girls on top of them clawing and pulling hair. The four of us were thrown into a cell together, where another fight broke out. But Preston and I got out first, so we won. Let's just say the sheriff learned there are usually separate holding cells for men and women for a reason.

"We won't get arrested," I finally agree.

"Mm-hmm, I've heard that a time or two," she says, but smiles because I think she knows it's as much fun as it looks. She never knows what we'll do next, because *we* don't even know what we'll do next. The shit we get into is never planned. It's all just passed on to us by destiny herself.

Is that your car I see? Preston texts.

I smile as I pick up my phone from the counter and reply. *Stalking me much?*

Keep your friends close. Keep your partner in crime closer, he replies.

I laugh. *I'm home. Come over.*

He doesn't respond, but a few minutes later, I hear Dad talking outside with someone. I stand up and move to the patio door, seeing Preston and my dad standing in the center of the brick pile.

A wide smile covers my face as I push my way out the door and run to him. He catches me in a big hug, pulling me against his chest as I wrap my legs around his hips.

"Damn, Pipes. Gained a few pounds?" he jokes.

I pull away and smack him hard across the chest. He quickly covers it with his hand and rubs the sore spot. "Don't be a jerk, asshole," I tell him.

He laughs. "I was only kidding. Who knew you were so sensitive about your weight? You look damn good to me," he says, eyes moving up and down my body, making that fire inside me burn hotter. "In fact, it looks like you've *lost* some weight."

"I thought so too," Mom says, coming to a stop beside me as she hands Preston a glass of lemonade.

"I haven't lost much," I argue. "I've just been staying busy with the magazine and working on the house."

"Thanks for the lemonade, Mrs. Montgomery," Preston says, lifting the glass and taking a drink.

"Anytime, dear. How's your brother doing? I haven't seen him in a long while."

He nods. "He's good. He's been busy with work since his new law office opened last month."

"That's right. I forgot all about that. We were invited to the grand opening, but I'd come down with a horrible cold and couldn't make it."

"See, Piper," Dad says, pointing at me, "Calvin's who you need to be settling down with. Stop messing around with punks."

I roll my eyes and laugh. Dad has never liked any of the guys I've dated. But he obviously can't pick them out any better than I can if he thinks I need to be with Calvin, my best friend's brother. "Yeah, yeah, I know, Dad," I agree without meaning a word of it.

Preston laughs. "I've never thought of that before. You and Calvin?" He erupts into a fit of laughter.

I frown. "What's so damn funny about Calvin and me? You don't think I deserve him?"

He waves his hand through the air. "You're complete opposites. I mean, he's always serious. You're never serious. You're like me: wild and free and just looking for fun."

He goes on comparing us and why I'd never work with his brother, but all I hear is how Preston and I would make the perfect couple. I wonder if he's even listening to himself talk. Does he really think we're alike? If he does, doesn't he see how perfect we'd be for each other? I mean, Calvin's idea of a good time is reading a book on a beach while sipping on some expensive cocktail. Preston and I would much rather be splashing in the water, partying, and nearly drinking ourselves to death on cheap keg beer. He's right: Calvin and I would never work.

"All right, you've proved your point. Now let's get to the bar and get a head start on Danny."

"Now you're making sense. See you later, Mr. and Mrs. M." He hands off the half-empty glass of lemonade before tapping my back. "You're it. Last one to the car buys the first round." He goes sprinting past me.

"Hey . . . cheater!" I yell, chasing after him.

As per the (unfair) bet, I buy the first pitcher of beer since he beat me to the car. We're sitting at our favorite booth in the back of Tino's Bar. The entire table is covered in fried food—fried pickles, a blooming onion, cheese sticks, and hot wings. Both of us are chowing down and chasing it with cheap beer.

"You remember that time we tried to see who could go the longest without drinking while we wolfed down the hottest wings this place had to offer?"

I laugh. "How could I forget? I couldn't leave the bathroom for days!"

He smiles wide. "Me neither. But I won."

"You did *not* win," I argue. "We both agreed to cave and drink at the same time."

"Yeah, but I had eight wings and you only had seven."

I roll my eyes. "It was a tie. We both agreed. Plus, if I *hadn't* agreed, you would've had to keep eating, and I don't think you could've choked down one more wing if your life depended on it."

"Yeah, yeah." He grabs a cheese stick and snaps off a bite, the cheese stringing from his mouth to his hand.

"Remember that spring break when we told our parents we were going to check out Calvin's college and ended up getting drunk on the beach in Florida?"

His eyes grow big around. "Fuck yeah. That was my first case of alcohol poisoning. I seriously thought I was going to die."

I giggle. "Yeah, I'm surprised they never found out about that."

"*My* parents did! But they wouldn't have if the bill hadn't come in the mail. I made them promise to keep it a secret from your parents since you basically saved my life by forcing my ass to go to the hospital."

I smile. "I don't know how my parents didn't figure out what we were up to. I mean, Calvin is four years older than us. Did they really think he'd be able to keep our asses in line when we visited his college?"

"Honestly, we were such a pain in the ass, they were probably just glad to get a break from us," he laughs out, and I agree.

"My mom told me we better not call them needing to get bailed out tonight."

He waves his hand through the air. "I think it's my parents' turn anyway. Remember, last time we got arrested because you threw your empty beer can at the cop as we were walking home."

My mouth drops open. "Don't blame me! I didn't know he was a cop. The car was unmarked. Plus you were the one who said he was following us because he wanted to throw my ass in the back of the car and take me away."

He laughs. "And I wasn't wrong, was I?"

I hold up my middle finger. "I thought it was because he was a creep, not a cop!" We both laugh. "I thought he was going to try to kidnap the drunk girl to sell on the dark web or something, not a cop who was going to arrest me for public intoxication and take me to jail, you asshole."

He laughs harder. "I never expected you to throw your beer can at him! And you screamed, 'You'll never catch me!' Then as he was cuffing you, you proceeded to yell about not wanting your liver sold on the black market and how it wasn't any good anyhow because you'd used it up," he laughs out.

"Shut up. I thought I was being abducted!"

He shakes his head at me as our laughing subsides. Danny walks in and plops down next to me. He pulls me roughly to his side and proceeds to grind his knuckles into the top of my head like someone might do with a younger sibling. "What's up, Pipes? Haven't seen you in forever."

I manage to push him away and land a solid punch to the top of his thigh. "Nothing much, Dan. How about you?"

He laughs as he rubs the spot. "Still got that right hook, I see."

I give him a beaming smile. "Hanging out with the two of you, I need my right hook to stay strong."

He smiles as I watch his eyes slowly fall down my face. They continue past my neck and land straight on my chest. I gasp as I smack him. "You're checking me out!"

"So what? I haven't seen you in, what, a year? You're looking good, Pipes."

I snort as I tip back my beer. Danny is good-looking by most people's standards. He's tall but not too tall. He's toned but not defined. He has shaggy dark hair and random tattoos. His dark eyes are beautiful, though, and he has that scruff on his jaw that I seem to be into lately. He's a player, though nothing compared to Preston's body count. He's a cool guy to hang out and drink with. In fact, I'm probably stupid for not having a thing for him like most of the girls did back in high school. But I have my eye on Preston and no one can compare.

"So, how are you and that douche doing anyhow?" Danny asks, looking over at me.

My brows pull together. "What douche?"

He scoffs before taking a long drink of beer. "The one who worked in advertising. He had blond hair and dressed like he was about to take out the sailboat after throwing his millions to the peasants."

I laugh at his description. "You mean Dean?"

"That's the one," he says, smiling toward Preston.

"I broke up with him, like, six months ago. How do you even know about him?" I try to think back to a time when I may have introduced them, but like Danny said, we haven't seen each other in a year and Dean and I only dated for about four months.

"Your boy told me." He gestures toward Preston.

I look over at him. "Why are you telling your friends my business?"

Danny laughs. "Oh, so I guess we're not friends now?"

"You know what I mean," I mumble, still waiting on an answer from Preston, but he looks like he's been caught in a lie.

"I didn't like the asshole. That's why."

"You only met him one time," I argue.

"Yeah, but I had to hear about him every time we talked. Felt like I was dating the guy," he laughs out.

I sit back and shake my head, picking up my beer and taking a drink. Part of me hopes that Preston was bothered by Dean because he secretly has a thing for me, but I'm not sure I can convince myself of that. I think back to all the times we've danced together, cuddled, or did anything else in close proximity . . . but he's never made a move. That speaks louder than anything else. If he wanted me, he would've made it known like he has with so many other girls. I need to let it go.

"Well, what about you and Tracy?" I ask Danny, needing to occupy my mind.

"We're still together. Going on 10 years now."

"What? No way! You guys fought worse than the two of us," I joke, nudging Preston.

"They still do," Preston says quietly.

Danny shoots him a look. "Yeah, we fight and argue. What couple doesn't? We've been together for a decade! But there's no way I'm putting that kind of time into training someone new." He smirks and I roll my eyes.

"Yeah, right. You mean you don't want to waste another 10 years getting retrained by another woman. That's what we do for you boys, you know. We whip you into shape in the hope of you being the one. When you're not, you move on to your next master."

Both guys take offense to that and they're booing me and trying to talk over me to prove their points, all while I sit back laughing.

As the hours pass, the beer goes down smoothly and we've even had a few shots. Danny is sitting next to me, telling me about his motorcycle business and how he plans to ask Tracy to marry him. Preston leans against the bar, hitting on his next conquest. I try my best to listen to Danny, but all I can focus on is Preston and the way he's looking at the woman he's talking to. His blue eyes are lit up like the sun is shining against them. He keeps offering her his flirty grin, wetting his lips to make them glisten. And every so often, he makes an excuse to lightly touch her: he's picked up the charm on her necklace, he's brushed imaginary lint off her shoulder, and he's even found an excuse to run the tip of his finger across her cheek. He's never done any of that with me.

If I had something on my face, he didn't brush it away for me. Most of the time he didn't even tell me because he thought it'd be funnier to watch me walk around like that. If he liked my necklace, he never reached out to touch it. He'd simply say, "Hey, cool necklace —which douchebag gave you that?" And as far as touching my shoulder or arm, he usually tackled me to the ground in an attempt to torture me. I've heard guys talk about being stuck in the friend zone, but I didn't realize it happened to girls.

I guess maybe I should start a friend zone club for girls. We could sit in a big circle, pass a bottle of wine, and tell each other about the guy who just couldn't see us as anything more than their friend. I'll call it *End Zone*. Get it? Like friEND, meaning the end of this bull-shit relationship we're stuck in.

But honestly, I don't want to end the relationship I have with Preston. I love him. He's my best friend and he knows all my secrets, even the embarrassing ones. If I have to pick between being his friend or nothing at all, I'll take what I can get. That's how in love I am. I'd rather sit on the sidelines and watch every other girl get the one thing I can't have over not having him in my life at all. I'm pathetic.

"Have you even listened to one word I've said?" Danny asks, interrupting my thoughts.

"Huh?" I ask, finally turning to look at him.

He looks from me, to Preston, and back. He lets out a light chuckle and shakes his head. "Still have that crush, huh?"

My back straightens. "What? What crush? What are you talking about?"

He roll his eyes. "Yeah, right," he mumbles as he takes a sip of his beer.

I bump my shoulder to his. "Seriously."

He sets his empty glass down and turns to look at me. "I see it, Piper. Everyone sees it. Well, except for him, I guess."

"Really?" I ask, feeling my face heat up. "He doesn't know? At all?"

"He's never mentioned it. You've never told him?"

"No way! I'm too afraid he'd turn me down. I mean, we're best friends. To him, I'm built like a Barbie doll down there."

He laughs. "I doubt that. You're built too nice up top to just have a lump in your jeans."

I bump against his arm again. "What do you think he'd say?"

He looks over at him again. "Honestly, I think he'd turn you down. But not because he doesn't think you're attractive or anything like that. I think you two have a relationship most people never get—something everyone wants. It doesn't matter if you're wrong; he will always have your back, because you'd do the same for him. He needs a constant in his life. And that's you. I don't think he'd ever do anything to jeopardize that. He needs you too much. He loves you too much to risk losing you."

I sit back, watching Preston, and nod.

"I'm going for a refill. Need anything?"

I shake my head as he walks away. Maybe he's right. Maybe I need to let this crush go and accept the fact that I won't ever have Preston the way I want. But I feel slightly better when I realize I already have him in a way no other woman ever will. Well, at least not until he gets married.

THREE

PIPER

Around midnight, the woman Preston's been working on gets up and leaves. He stands back and watches her go with a smile. When she's no longer in sight, he makes his way back to the table.

"Aw, leaving empty-handed?" Danny teases him.

"Yeah, but I got her number," Preston says, holding a piece of paper between his index and middle finger. He tucks it into his pocket before looking over at me. "You about ready to call it a night? If you drink much more, I have a feeling we'll be making that call to my parents." He gives me a smile—a smile that's reserved only for friends.

I nod. "Yeah, let's do it." I finish off my beer as he works his way out of the booth. When my glass is gone, I push myself up. The fast movement goes straight to my head. Dizziness takes over and I trip on my own feet, falling straight into his arms.

He's smiling wide at my clumsiness but helps get me to my feet. "Whoa, guess it's a good thing we're leaving. Someone has gotten weak on us, Dan."

"Screw you. I'm not weak and I hold my alcohol just fine. I just

THE WRONG BROTHER   21

tripped over the table leg," I lie. Truth is, I don't drink as much as I used to. I find there's no time in my life for hangovers.

"Yeah, okay. Let's get you home," Preston says, agreeing but sounding like he's only doing so to keep me under control.

I smile and wave. "Bye, Danny."

He laughs and shakes his head at me. "See ya next time, Pipes."

Preston leads me out to his car in the parking lot. He opens my door and helps me down into the seat. I buckle up while he walks around the car and gets behind the wheel.

"Wait, aren't you drunk? Should we walk again?" I ask.

He laughs. "I'm not drunk. I haven't had a drink since that first pitcher, and that was, like, four hours ago."

"What?" I ask, confused. Wasn't he right there drinking beside me the whole time? Well, he was with that woman for a while. A lonnnnnng while. Now that I think of it, he didn't have a drink that whole time. And he didn't share any of the pitchers Danny bought. No wonder I'm so drunk. Danny and I had at least three pitchers to ourselves.

"This is your fault." I point at him.

He laughs. "What's my fault?"

"Me being this drunk. I'm going to have a hangover tomorrow because of you."

"How's it my fault?" he asks, turning out of the parking lot.

"I thought you were drinking with me. Turns out, I drank twice as much as I thought because you weren't drinking your share."

He laughs harder. "You would still be this drunk, dumbass. We just would've spent more money."

Oh. Yeah, I guess he's right. When I start drinking, I don't like to stop until something *makes* me stop: I get sick, I pass out, or the bar closes. I'm many things, but I'm not a quitter. Which is another reason I don't drink very often anymore.

"My mom's going to be sooo mad at me when I get home," I laugh out.

"At least you didn't get arrested," he points out.

"Good point! I'll make sure to bring that up if she starts yelling at me."

"Any plans for tomorrow?" he asks, glancing at me from the corner of his eye.

I shrug. "Nothing on the books yet. Why, what's up?"

"I was thinking we could have a good old-fashioned beach day— you know, like we used to? We could pack a cooler then spend the day working on our tans and getting drunk. Then we could grab some dinner off the hot dog cart. Sound good?"

I smile, thinking about all the good times we've had on our beach days. "Sounds good! Noon? You know I don't like getting up early, and now that you've got me this drunk, it'll probably be even harder to get out of bed."

"Noon it is," he agrees as he pulls into the drive at my parents' house.

I unbuckle and climb out. Like the gentleman he doesn't want anyone to know he is, he waits until I get inside the house before backing out of the drive. I bounce my way off the walls up to my room. The second I fall into bed, the only thing I can think about is my Uncle Peter and my Aunt Beth getting it on in my room, around my things . . . in front of my baby picture, for crying out loud! First thing tomorrow, I'll be telling Mom to buy a new bed. This one's tainted.

———

MY PHONE RINGS and pulls me out of a deep sleep—so deep I didn't have one nightmare about my tainted bed. I grab it off the bedside table and answer it without looking.

"Hello?"

"Rise and shine, sunshine," Preston says, sounding way too cheerful for as bad as I feel.

I don't respond. I can only groan.

"Oh, come on. We have a day full of festivities planned. Get your ass up and let's hit the beach."

"I thought we agreed to noon?"

"It's 11:30. By the time you get ready, it'll be past noon. Now get up. Don't make me pick you up out of bed. You know I will."

"Fine. I'm getting up." I hang up the phone and go directly to the connected bathroom, hoping a shower will make me feel more human. A good 30 minutes later, I'm climbing out and pulling on my red bikini. I tie it extra tight with the memory of Preston running by me on the beach and snagging the string, causing the bottom half to untie on one side. I remember my face was just as red as this bathing suit.

I pull my honey-blonde hair into a messy bun, tug on my shorts, and slide on my flip-flops. For good measure, I grab my extra-dark sunglasses before exiting my room. I find him already in the living room, talking with my parents as they watch TV.

"There she is," my dad says when he sees me walking down the stairs.

"Morning," I mumble.

"Morning? Ha!" Dad scoffs. "You're just as irresponsible as you were at 16."

I wrinkle my nose at him. "Don't judge me. I'm on vacation."

That causes my parents to laugh.

"Ready to go?" Preston asks. "A warm muffin and some coffee await you in the car."

"Mmm, I'm ready," I agree, a little too eagerly.

Preston opens the door for me and the moment I step out, I'm blinded by bright sunlight. My head throbs as I shield my eyes, causing me to walk right into my mom's ceramic planter. "Oweee!" I cry as I jump up and down on one foot while holding my shin with both hands.

Preston laughs. "Come on, vampire. I'll get your blind ass to the car." He places his hands on my shoulders and leads me off the porch toward the car. Once inside, the tinted windows make opening my eyes much easier. I look down at my shin to see a scrape and a bruise already forming.

When he takes his seat, I turn my heated gaze on him.

"What? It's not my fault you hurt yourself," he says around a grin.

He's right, but that doesn't stop me from being mad at him. He starts the car and I sit back, pulling my seatbelt over my body. "Where's my muffin?" I ask, looking around the car and not seeing my favorite white, blue, and yellow bag.

He rolls his eyes but reaches into the back seat, handing over the bag. I smile as I open it, peeking inside to see my favorite banana nut muffin. I inhale the sweet scent and my mouth instantly waters.

As he starts driving toward the beach, I tear off the top of the muffin and put a small piece into my mouth. It practically melts on my tongue. I lean my head back, close my eyes, and smile, enjoying the sweetness. "Mmmmm," I moan. "It's literally like heaven in my mouth."

He snickers and shakes his head. "If only I could find a woman who treats me as well as you treat your baked goods, we'd all be set."

I glance at him from the corner of my eye. *Um, hello! She's right here! You think I treat my baked goods well, you should see how well I'd treat you. It wouldn't be a muffin melting on my tongue right now. It would be your hard coc . . .*

"Should we swing by the store to grab stuff for a picnic or live off hot dogs all day?" he asks, interrupting my thoughts.

I feel my face heating up. It's like he knew what I was thinking and wanted to stop it before it could go too far. "I'm good eating wieners all day," I say around a smile as I wag my brows at him.

He laughs and pushes against my arm. "There is seriously something wrong with you."

"What's the most wieners you've ever eaten in one sitting?"

He shakes his head. "Can we stop calling them wieners?"

"Fine. How many hot dogs can you eat in one sitting?" I need a distraction and, hey, I'm always willing to talk about winning that hot dog eating contest a few months back.

He shrugs. "I guess four?"

"Four?" I scoff. "Amateur."

He laughs in disbelief. "Okay, big shot. How many have you eaten?"

"Seventeen!" I gloat.

He laughs even harder. "What? No fucking way. I'm hitting the bullshit button on that one."

"I swear. And I have proof!" I grab my phone and pull up the picture that was taken of me after I won the contest. My stomach is probably double its normal size. My cheeks are puffed out like a squirrel carrying nuts, I have a sash across my chest, and both arms are thrust into the air, ecstatic I won. Next to me is a judge holding a sign with the number 17 on it. He's also holding an envelope containing my prize.

He looks at the picture and laughs. "If I were you, I wouldn't be proud of this. Delete that shit and deny it if anyone asks if it's you."

I smack his arm. "Are you kidding me? I'm thinking about having it framed. This is my finest hour!"

He chuckles and looks toward the road. "What did you win anyway?"

"Free Netflix for a year," I state.

His mouth drops open. "You ate 17 hot dogs, probably made yourself sick, and took a year off your life for a one-year subscription to Netflix?"

I smile and nod. "And bragging rights, of course!"

"My statement still stands." There's a long, drawn-out silence as I put my phone away and he continues to drive. "What made you join a hot dog eating contest to begin with?"

I smile. "My friend Riley and I went to the state fair. We had tickets to a concert, but we went early just to hang out, drink, and stuff our faces with fair food. Anyway, we got hammered in the beer garden and needed to sober up before the concert, so we went in search of food. We were passing by the hot dog eating contest stand and she bet me I wouldn't do it. I figured, two birds, one stone. I got free food and I won the bet! And a year of free Netflix! Triple win!"

"And that's why we're friends," he laughs out. "You see what I mean about you and Calvin never working out? He would never even consider doing something like that. And here you are, doing it just to prove a point."

I snort. "Not that I would ever even consider dating your brother, but am I really that different from him? And if I am, people do say that opposites attract. Maybe he's what I need and I'm what he needs. You know, he needs someone to push him to do something out of the box, and I need someone to keep me from crossing the line, because you know the line and I have never seen eye-to-eye."

He shrugs. "I guess you could be right, but what the hell would the two of you talk about?"

I bite my lower lip, desperate to prove my point. Don't ask me what my point is, because even I'm not sure. "Anything. The same things *we* talk about. I mean, you and I are exactly alike. We would have fun doing anything and everything. But Calvin and I would have to connect on a deeper level. Well, either that or he'd just have to be really good in bed," I joke, but he doesn't laugh. It's like he's too focused on something else, so I let the topic fall away completely.

A little while later, we make it to the beach and he grabs our things and carries them down to the sand. While he sets up the blanket, I stick the umbrella into the sand and get everything situated. I set up our beach chairs, strip out of my shorts, and place the cooler between our two chairs so neither of us has to reach far for a beer. I know beer is the last thing I should be thinking about after last night, but the hair of the dog is the only way I'm getting through this.

I take a seat in the chair and grab a beer. I slide on a koozie and pop the top, taking a long drink. Alcohol isn't allowed on the beach, but everyone does it, and as long as things don't get crazy and you're not openly showing your container, no one gives a shit.

Preston sits beside me and does the same. We both drink our beer and look out over the water. "Remember the graduation party we had here?"

I smile. "Of course I do. I finally got the chance to show up stupid Linda Miller by doing that keg stand and winning the party."

"Winning the party? That's what you think you did?" I can hear the amusement in his voice, so I turn to look at him with my brows drawn together.

"Yeah, what do you think I did?"

He smirks. "If I remember correctly, you did a keg stand, got dizzy and drunk, then puked on half the student body."

Oh yeah. I forgot about that part. "But after that, I did another keg stand and didn't puke. Still sounds like I won."

He laughs. "I love how you always make everything so positive. It's like that time I got into that fight and was suspended from the football game. You came over and we ended up getting trashed and going skinny-dipping in the pool."

I nod. "I remember that well. That was the first time I got to see little Preston." I laugh because I know the only word he'll focus on is *little*.

"Little? What do you mean little? If anything deserved the title of 'little,' it was your tits."

I gasp. "My tits were not little. They were still growing. I was a late bloomer. The same couldn't be said about you, though. Your voice changed in the sixth grade. One day you sounded normal and the next it sounded like you got ahold of Chewy's squeaky toy and had it lodged in your throat." I can't hold back my laugh when I think of a 12-year-old Preston chasing after the dog to get the squeaky toy from him.

"Shut up. It wasn't that bad." He playfully smacks my leg.

I nod. "Oh, it *was* that bad. I remember you trying to talk your mom into letting you skip school until it calmed down."

He shakes his head, annoyed that this is what we're talking about. "You think mine was bad? Don't you remember Calvin's?"

I honestly can't say that I do. By that point, Calvin was too old to hang out with us, since we were just a couple of kids at the time. He still hung out with us, but more in secret. I don't think he wanted to let on to his friends that he was slumming it with some dorky kids. "I don't think anyone was as bad as you, Pres."

He waves his hand through the air, done with this conversation. After a while, he asks, "So, how's work going?"

I nod as I take a sip of my beer, already starting to feel a little better. "It's going well. I've officially been there a year, so hopefully the promotions start rolling in soon."

"I don't understand the whole promotion thing. I mean, you're a writer now, so a promotion to what exactly?"

"Writing better pieces—things that make the cover or are a page long instead of just a couple paragraphs. The bigger the piece, the more recognition you get. And eventually, I could move to head writer—or even editor. However, it's going to take a lot longer than a year. Some people have been there since the magazine started, and they haven't even gotten a promotion yet." I shrug. "But for now, I'm content. I mean, it keeps me busy, it pays the bills, and I do enjoy writing." I look over at him as he watches a couple of girls run to the water. "How's work going for you?"

"Working on the Chicago Cubs team is cool, but being a systems analyst is kind of boring. It's all just a bunch of numbers and computer stuff, you know?"

I nod but don't understand a thing about his job. Preston went to college for sports management after dislocating his shoulder playing football our senior year. He wasn't ever super-serious about continuing to play in college, but I think part of him was hoping for a scholarship that would eventually take him to the NFL. When playing sports got thrown out the window, he went into sports management as a last resort to stay involved in sports even though he would never be a famous quarterback. I thought he loved his job, but it sounds like he just loves sports and wants to be involved however he can.

"And how's Calvin doing with his new law office?"

He nods and takes a sip. "Good, as far as I know. We only talk about once a week and it's rarely about work. I can tell you what he had for dinner last Thursday or that he just broke up with the woman he was seeing these last three months, but I don't know anything about his office or how it's going."

I smile. "Yeah, Jake and I are the same way. He just moved from his apartment in Chicago to his new place in New York. He got a big promotion with the move and my parents are so proud of him. Kinda leaves me feeling a little like a failure."

He studies my face. "You know that isn't true, right?"

I shrug. "I mean, Jake is some bigwig in the insurance industry and I'm a columnist? Doesn't really compare."

"And my brother is a lawyer and all I do is play with computers. When you say it like that, there's no comparison. But when I say I'm a systems analyst for the Chicago Cubs, it sounds a little better, don't you think?"

I laugh and nod. "You got me there. But there isn't any other way to say you're a columnist . . ."

"You could say you're the head writer for *Wonder Home Magazine*." His blue eyes widen and his brows shoot up like he's found the secret code.

I laugh. "But that isn't true. I'm not the head writer. I'm a lowly columnist."

He shrugs it off. "Maybe our bothers are the ones who need to get together. They're both outshining us."

I smile over at him. "You do realize my brother is married with a wife and three kids, right? I highly doubt there's any chance of that happening."

He looks offended that I shot down his idea. "You never know. He could still be hiding the truth from himself," he jokes.

"When are you going back home?" I ask him.

"Monday morning. You?"

"Tomorrow. I have work on Monday. You need to bring Calvin by my place. I haven't seen him in forever. Last Christmas, I think." I wrinkle my nose as I try to think of the last time I saw him.

"You got the hots for my brother?" he jokingly asks.

I snort and roll my eyes. "Highly doubtful," I laugh out and shrug. "The three of us haven't been together since Christmas. And other than holidays, it's been since, what, that spring break in Florida?"

He nods. "Yeah, I think so. He's usually only ever home for holidays and family functions. But now that he's in the city with us, we should all get together for old times' sake. I'll call him later and we'll set something up."

Preston, Calvin, and I used to hang out all the time before Calvin went off to college. If one of us went somewhere, we had the other two with us. My brother wasn't ever really part of the gang though. My brother is 10 years older than me. By the time I was old enough to do things, he was already out of the house and living his own life. Preston always used to give me shit and say I was the midlife crisis baby, but really, I think I was the glue that held our family together. Dad was always at work and Jake was old enough to do this own thing. That left our mom lonely and in need of someone to care for. That's where I came in. I'm the baby of the family and wouldn't have it any other way.

"Wanna play some volleyball?"

I smile wide. "You know it!" I finish off my beer and jump up, grabbing the ball and taking off toward the net. I stand on one side while Preston stands on the other. I throw the ball up and pull back my right fist, serving the ball. It flies over the net. Preston jumps forward, bumping the ball back to me before falling into the sand on his chest and stomach.

I run across the sand and bump it back, wobbling on my legs as I slide on the sand, but I manage to stay upright. The ball soars to the other side of the net and Preston can't get up in time. It lands on the sand only a few feet away from him.

"Ha! One-zero," I gloat.

He rolls his eyes but stands up and brushes off some sand before picking up the ball and tossing it to me to serve again. For several minutes, we manage to keep the ball in the air, but we're both hot, tired, and covered in sweat and sand. Someone has to give up or we're both going to fall over from exhaustion. I tap the ball over the net and Preston is right there, ready to spike it back to me. It's so fast, I don't even see it coming. The next thing I know, the ball is smashing against my face and I find myself on my back in the hot sand, pain radiating from my nose. I feel something wet and reach up to touch it. I pull my hand away with blood on my fingertips.

"Oh, shit! Pipes, are you okay?" he asks, rushing under the net and stopping at my side. He grabs my arm and helps me as I try to sit up.

"Is it broken?" I ask in a nasally voice as tears roll down my cheeks from the pain.

He gets right in front of my face and looks at it. "I don't think so. It's not crooked or anything. Come on, let's get you cleaned up." He takes my arm and pulls me to my feet.

He walks me back over to my chair and sits me down before handing me a napkin. "I'll go find a baggie and we'll get some ice on it so it doesn't swell."

I hold the napkin to my nose and lean my head back, trying to push past the pain.

Moments later, he's back with a sandwich baggie. He opens the cooler and grabs a handful of ice. He zips it closed and hands it over. I take the bag of ice and hold it to my nose.

"I swear, if I have black eyes, I'm going to kill you," I threaten.

He holds out a beer. "Peace offering?"

I take the beer roughly, snatching it out of his hand as I say, "Yes to the beer, no to the peace!"

He hangs his head. "I'm sorry. It was an accident. How about a hot dog?"

I crack open the beer and take a long drink, hoping the alcohol helps to numb the pain. "I want a hot dog and ice cream, and you have to do everything I say for the rest of the day. Deal?"

He laughs. "What? No way!"

"Then no peace for you." I take another sip and turn my attention to the water.

"Ugh," he groans. "Fine, my queen." *My queen* is what I always made Calvin and him call me when we were little. This trick isn't new. In fact, the two of them took turns being my royal servant throughout our childhood for various reasons, mostly because I got hurt in the middle of the boys' roughhousing.

I turn to look at him with a smile, happy that he's remembered this game so well. "That's more like it. I'm getting hungry. I'll take my wiener now," I tease.

"I thought we agreed to call it a hot dog?"

"We did, but I've changed my mind and now you must also call it a wiener for the rest of the day."

He stands and walks toward the snack stand, grumbling under his breath about hoping I choke on my wiener. I can't do anything but drink my beer with a smile. And on the plus side, my nose has stopped bleeding already. Looks like I win this day!

I wonder if I could maybe use this to my advantage. Perhaps I could get a kiss out of the deal, but that would probably tell him the one thing I've never been able to bring myself to say and my secret would be ruined . . . probably along with our friendship.

No, I won't out myself today, but I'm sure as shit going to take advantage of this situation. I smile to myself as he walks back over.

He holds out his hand with his head bowed forward. "Your wiener, my queen."

FOUR

PIPER

I eat my wiener and move on to strawberry ice cream in a waffle cone. I wash all of it down with more beer. Preston is acting as my gopher. He goes for bottled water I don't drink, sunblock I don't use, and a bag of cotton candy I don't eat. I hate cotton candy. It's sickly-sweet, sticky, and gross, but Preston doesn't need to know that. He does everything without complaint—well, he mumbles under his breath as he's walking away, but other than that, there's no complaining.

The two of us sit on the beach, talking, tanning, and swimming when we get too hot. He cuts back on drinking because he's too afraid to leave his car here overnight. So once again, I'm left drinking alone. By the time the sun is going down, I'm completely trashed and no help when it comes to picking up our belongings to leave.

Preston folds up his chair and I stand to do the same, but I can't get it to fold. I push and push, but it's not folding.

He laughs. "Get out of the way before you hurt yourself." He steps up to the chair, pushes a couple little buttons, and it easily folds up. He grabs the cooler and chairs and walks them to his car while I stuff my things into my bag. I grab my pair of shorts and step one foot into them. As I lift the other foot, I lose my balance and fall over. Thanks to the tanning lotion, sand is stuck to the entire right side of my body.

He walks back over to me with a smirk. "Seriously, you can't even dress yourself?"

"That's none of your business. Maybe this is how I get dressed every morning," I say, getting up on my feet and tugging my shorts into place.

He chuckles. "It probably is. Everyone knows you're not the most graceful person on the planet." He grabs the blanket up off the ground and it sends bits of sand in every direction, only covering me further.

At this point, what does it even matter? I'm pretty sure I have sand where the sun doesn't shine, but at least the ordeal has resulted in a nice tan. And maybe some black eyes. I've been too afraid to look.

We make the journey back to the car and I fall into the passenger seat, completely exhausted from the sun and drinking all day. Not to mention, having a hangover and not enough sleep. He climbs behind the wheel and starts up the car.

"Your mom is going to hate me if I keep bringing you home drunk," he laughs out.

I wave off his concerns. "Again, at least we didn't get arrested," I point out. No matter what we do, as long as we don't get arrested, we're doing well. At least in her eyes.

Traffic is heavy on the ride home and we're moving at a snail's pace. I'm tempted to grab another beer out of the cooler in the back seat, but Preston already told me he'd break my fingers if I tried. He said we're too close to home to get arrested for having an open container in a moving vehicle.

His phone rings and Calvin's name pops up on the car display.

"Hey, man. What's up?" Preston answers by pushing a button on the steering wheel.

"Hi, Calvin!" I scream.

Calvin lets out a deep, raspy chuckle that has my stomach tightening. *What was that?* I've never had that tingling from Calvin before.

"Hey, Piper. You sound wasted. My brother being a bad influence again?"

"Hey, I've been good this weekend. It's Piper who's the bad influence. She's been drunk all weekend."

My mouth drops open as my eyes widen at him. How dare he throw me under the bus! He's the one providing the alcohol!

"Only because you insisted," I point out.

Calvin laughs. "You two seriously need a leash, you know that? It's like the blind leading the blind."

I shrug and Preston tilts his head to the side like he's considering Calvin's words.

"Anyway, I just wanted to see what you two were up to tonight. I don't have any work to do and all my buddies went on a whitewater rafting trip without me because I had a business dinner, which just fell through. I'm on my way home if you want to hang out."

"Yeah, that sounds good. We're leaving the beach now. How far out are you?" Preston asks.

"About an hour," Calvin answers.

"That gives us just enough time to get cleaned up. We'll have dinner and find some kind of trouble to get into," Preston says, smiling at me.

"Pres, I'm a lawyer. My troublemaking days are over. But dinner sounds good. I'll see you in a bit." Without a goodbye, he hangs up.

I don't know why, but I'm suddenly feeling awkward about seeing Calvin again. And what was that tingle that came over me when I heard him laugh? Calvin has always been good-looking, and by good-looking I mean he's drop-dead sexy just like Preston. The Young men are luckier than most and their genes are amazing. I guess I just never saw Calvin that way because he was so much older than us. He's only four years older, but growing up, that may as well have been a lifetime. He was leaving high school just as we were getting started.

He and Preston look a lot alike. They both have dark hair and icy blue eyes. Calvin is just a little taller than Preston though, and he's more cut than bulky when it comes to muscles. Calvin is more lean and cut where Preston is thicker.

The thing that always had me on team Preston, though, was how differently they acted. Preston is wild and free and always down to have fun despite the cost. Calvin is more responsible. He never does anything without giving it serious thought and making a pros and cons list. Preston grows out his beard, goes months without a haircut, and dresses in whatever he grabs in the morning. Calvin wears expensive suits, always keeps his facial hair trimmed low to the skin, and his dark hair is always neatly styled. One brother is always lax and chill while the other is uptight and serious. Clearly, I've always leaned toward relaxing and having fun.

I've been so lost in my mental comparison of Preston and Calvin that I didn't realize we were already pulling into Preston's parents' driveway. He looks over at me and his brows pull together. "Are you sick? You look a little funny."

I wipe the expression off my face. Sick. Yes, I'm feeling sick! I think I just got turned on by Calvin's laugh! I need to get away from him before he figures this out. "I'm fine. I'm going to go shower." I quickly get out of the car before heading across the street to my parents' house.

I speed walk straight to the front door. Once I step inside and close it behind me, I lean my back against it while I catch my breath. I don't know what's wrong with me. It's probably just a little mix of confusion due to drinking all day, getting hit in the face with a volleyball, and too much sun. Hell, maybe I have a concussion.

I hear my mom banging around in another room, so I walk through the living room to the kitchen, where she's loading the dishwasher.

She looks up at me and smiles. "Hey, hon. How was the beach?"

"Preston drilled me in the face with a volleyball he spiked at me. You think I have a concussion or a broken nose?"

She steps closer, looking over my face carefully. After a moment of staring into my eyes, she says, "I think you'll survive. I have some really good foundation that should cover that black eye though."

Black eye? I take off running toward my room. I push open the door and come to a sudden stop in front of the mirror hanging above my dresser. I lean forward, needing a closer look. My eyes are blood-shot and glassy—probably from drinking—and there are dark circles under them from a lack of rest and water, but I don't see a black eye. I breathe out a sigh of relief.

"Ha! Gotcha!" Mom yells up.

I roll my eyes and shake my head. What's wrong with my family?

I close my bedroom door and head for the bathroom to wash the sand out of a place that should never be sandy.

An hour later, I'm showered, dressed, and have my hair and makeup done perfectly. I've forced myself to drink plenty of water and am finally starting to feel like a living member of society again rather than some drunk alley rat.

I stand back and look myself over in the mirror. I have no idea what kind of night Preston is planning for the three of us, but I know I want to look good. I don't want to dress for a baseball game only to be taken to a nice restaurant two towns over, so I think the summer dress I picked out will work for any situation. It'll be cool if we go to any outside event, but it still looks nice and dressy if we go someplace a little more fancy. The summer dress is white and made out of layered lace. It's form-fitting and ends a little above my knee. I've paired the dress with a pair of sandals and left my hair hanging down my back in soft curls.

I didn't want to cake my face with makeup just to sweat it off if we'll be outside, so all I'm wearing is a little lip gloss and mascara. The sun I got today did wonders for my no-makeup look. My cheeks are slightly pink from spending the day on the beach, and my skin is slightly darker, making me look fresh and well-rested.

My phone chimes from the bed and I quickly grab it to read the screen. *We're ready to go. Get your ass over here.*

I roll my eyes with a smile and tuck my phone into a small purse before starting toward the door. As I'm walking across the street toward Preston's car, the two of them come walking out of the house. I nearly stop in my tracks when I see them. Oh, what girl wouldn't fantasize about having both of them? Preston is dressed in dark wash jeans and a fitted blue T-shirt. He's wearing his Cubs hat that shades his blue eyes, and he hasn't touched that dark scruff on his jaw. My mouth waters.

Calvin isn't dressed in his usual suit. He's wearing a pair of jeans that hug his narrow hips nicely. He's wearing a white T-shirt that doesn't fit as tightly as Preston's. What I notice most, though, is his red Cardinals hat.

I smile as I close the distance between us. I point to his hat when he notices me walking up. "What the hell is that? You live in Chicago and you're sporting merch for St. Louis?"

He smiles wide but pulls me in for a hug. "Hey, I did live there for three years, you know. And, well, they have a better team."

I inhale his scent. It's deep and rich and smells expensive. "Did you hear that, Pres?"

"Yeah, I heard the traitor," he says, looking at him from the other side of the car. I giggle because even I felt the heat from his glare.

"Yeah, yeah," Calvin says, placing his hand on my lower back as he opens the car door for me. Normally, an innocent act like this wouldn't even register with me, but after that flood of tingles earlier, I can't help but notice every little thing. And the strangest part is that with his touch, the tingles seem to take over my body again.

I climb into the back seat, leaving Preston and Calvin to sit up front. I know, how sweet of me to give up the front seat so easily. Honestly, I needed to hide away. I need to figure this out. No way could I develop a crush on a guy I haven't even seen in six months. God, spending all this time with Preston is screwing with my head. That has to be it. When I'm around him, my body is on high alert. I must have some wires crossed inside me, because they're not just picking up on Preston. Now they're picking up on Calvin too.

I shake the thoughts from my head. Calvin is the same guy he's always been. While Preston was the one I'd go to when I wanted to have fun or cause a little trouble, I went to Calvin with my problems: I liked a guy and didn't know how to tell him how I felt, or I got a bad grade and needed help bringing it up before my parents found out. Sometimes we just talked about what was going on in my life. He never offered up much information about his own life, but he's always been by my side to help me through whatever storm I was caught up in. There's nothing and there will never be anything other than friendship between Calvin and me. I mentally dust off my hands—done with the whole situation.

A little while later, we're pulling up to a sports-bar-style restaurant a town over. The parking lot is packed and the restaurant is even worse. Nearly every table is filled, and the room's so loud it's deafening.

"Table for three, please," Preston tells the hostess.

She grabs three menus and walks us over to a table in the corner. While it's busy and crowded, we end up with a great table, because there's a TV on every side of us. One's playing a baseball game, one has an old football game on, one has some sort of MMA fight, and the last one is playing an old basketball game.

The three of us take our seats and Preston orders a pitcher of beer for the table. I glance over the menu until the pitcher and three glasses are set down. Preston grabs the pitcher and starts pouring some in each glass.

He hands me mine and I take a sip, watching as Calvin raises his glass and takes a drink. I smile, wondering if he's going to manage to choke down the cheap beer, but he looks at me, confused.

"What?"

I shrug. "I was just waiting to see if you could choke it down, Mr. Grey Goose."

The corners of his mouth lift up slightly. He rolls his icy eyes. "I can drink beer with the best of them."

I arch one eyebrow. "Last time you decided to drink beer with us, you ended up puking it all up in the women's porta-potty."

Preston laughs but quickly stops when Calvin cuts him with his gaze.

"What can I say? My body prefers higher quality than most." He gives me his cocky, lopsided grin and my heart flutters.

Damn this body of mine! What's wrong with you? This is Calvin. We don't react this way to Calvin! We laugh at Calvin for being prissy and uptight. We make fun of Calvin for thinking he's better than us. We don't get goo-goo eyes for Calvin. We don't get tingles. And our heart most certainly doesn't flutter from a grin he shoots us.

I realize I'm biting my inner cheek when I detect the metallic taste of blood. I release it and pick up my beer, gulping it down quickly. I turn my attention to Preston and smile as I watch the way he moves. The way his eyes squint as he and Calvin talk between themselves. The way he has little dimples that appear when he laughs. I notice his arm flex as he picks up the pitcher and pours more beer in our glasses, and the way his eyes quickly glance at me as a way of saying *you're welcome*. My heart picks up again and I finally feel like everything is back to normal.

As I watch him and all the little movements he makes, I find myself squeezing my thighs together as a flood of want settles over me. Why is this man so hot? How can he control my body so easily without even knowing it?

The waitress comes to take our order, and of course, both gentlemen look over at me to order first. I smile at their politeness and pick up my menu, reading off my choice. "I'll take six boneless wings with hot sauce, an order of seasoned fries with queso cheese on the side, and another pitcher."

She writes it down before looking at Preston. "That sounds good," he says. "I'll have the same but give me 12 wings with fire sauce." He hands over his menu as the waitress looks at Calvin.

He grows quiet as he studies the menu before finally ordering. "I'll just take a salad with any low-fat dressing you have. Also, I'd like it topped with low-fat shredded cheese. No bacon bits or croutons."

I can't help the way my mouth drops open by his healthy order. He looks at me, amused. "What?"

"We're at a freaking sports bar. You're supposed to order beer, wings, burgers, or anything fried, and you order the healthiest salad on the menu?" I ask, making Preston laugh.

Calvin rolls his eyes. "You two are going to die in your 50s, whereas I'll still be kicking till I'm 90. Then we'll see who ordered correctly."

I wave my hand through the air and sit back in my chair.

Preston leans in and whispers in my ear. "We might die sooner but I know who's going to have more fun."

I smirk at his statement and Calvin rolls his eyes but doesn't argue. Probably because he knows it's true.

"How's the new office going, Calvin?" I ask, wanting to distract myself from these boys.

He offers up a smile. "Everything is great. We're staying busy. How's your job?"

I cock my head to the side. "Where do I work, Calvin?"

He looks nervous. He's never once asked me about my job. "Uhh, some magazine, right?"

I scoff. "Yes, I work for a magazine and it's great. Thanks for asking."

Preston laughs and shakes his head. "She's been there for a year, man. You still don't know where she works?"

He shrugs. "There are a ton of magazines out there and I don't read any of them. So no, I'm not up-to-date on magazines. Forgive me."

I pick up my glass and take another swig. "It's fine, Calvin. It's not like we really keep in touch anymore anyway."

He opens his mouth to say something but quickly snaps it closed when the waitress is back with another pitcher. Preston pours the almost-empty one into our glasses and hands it over so she can set down the fresh beer.

"Where we going after this?" I ask, taking a drink.

Preston shrugs. "Bar?"

I smile and nod while Calvin looks a little annoyed that he agreed to join this gang of miscreants.

"Boomers? We can fight to the death with a game of shuffle-board!" Preston and I always go head-to-head in a game of shuffle-board. "Calvin, you down?" I ask.

He presses his lips together tightly, thinking it over. "I don't know. I'm more of a darts man."

"Oh, come on. Don't be a stick-in-the-mud."

"All right, fine," he agrees. "I'll take winner."

"Yes!" I softly cheer, doing a little dance in my seat.

The waitress brings over our food and I immediately dig in, running a fry through the cheese and popping it into my mouth. The delicious taste has me wiggling in my seat once again with a little happy dance. Both the guys laugh and shake their heads at me.

"I wish I could be that happy with just food," Preston says.

Calvin snorts. "Clearly, she's had too much to drink today, Preston."

Preston laughs and waves him off. "She's fine. I've been with her the whole time."

I nod as I pick up another fry. "It's true, Cal. Even after he spiked a volleyball at my face! Which reminds me . . ."

"Oh shit. I thought you forgot," Preston breathes out.

I giggle. "Get ready to have some fun, Cal, cause Preston is all mine tonight."

Calvin laughs. "Please tell me you two aren't still doing that royal servant shit?"

"Oh, we're doing it. Too bad I didn't remember sooner. You'd be having nothing but wieners for dinner, Pres."

He silently chuckles beside me as he picks up a wing and tosses it into his mouth.

My mind is already spinning through the possibilities. Tonight's bar trip will be epic. Now, how can I punish Preston?

FIVE

CALVIN

Piper fucking Montgomery. God, if you only knew all the dirty thoughts I've had about my little brother's best friend, you'd probably think I was some kind of pervert. I mean, who's not attracted to this woman—other than my dumbass brother? She's absolutely gorgeous with her long honey-blonde hair that's always done up perfectly in soft curls. She's tall—nearly as tall as I am—and she's thin while having all the soft curves a man craves. She's funny and smart and fun, and I know her in a way that even my brother doesn't.

She and Preston have been the best of friends since we were kids. They're so alike—two peas in a pod. I'm the complete opposite. While they were busy having fun and going to parties, I was focusing on passing the bar. I've always looked toward the future, wanting to make sure I set up my life the way I'd envisioned it. But here I am, right where I wanted to be, with my own law office, and I'm completely alone. On the career side of things, I have everything I've always wanted. But on a more personal level, I'm still right where she left me years ago. All alone while she ran off to play with my little brother.

I've watched her grow into the woman she is now. I've watched her pine for my brother, who's never seemed to notice the little crush she's always had on him. I've let her cry on my shoulder when she's had to watch him go out with every other girl but her. I've given her advice on how to get over him. I've held her hand when she's needed strength. Yet she's never seen me as anything but Preston's older, boring brother.

I've never told anyone this, but she's the reason I left and moved to St. Louis for a few years. I couldn't stand back and watch her chase after him any longer. I couldn't watch her choose the wrong brother time and time again. She's so blinded by her feelings for him that she can't see my feelings for her. I mean, I never came right out and said it, but that's because I knew how she'd respond. She'd probably run off and tell Preston, who would come to me all kinds of pissed off. I know my brother loves her, but he's not *in* love with her. He won't allow himself to be. He needs her too much and he won't risk losing her by starting up anything serious. He'd also be afraid I'd screw things up for them.

But as I sit here and watch her watch him, it twists at my insides. Preston and I have talked about Piper before. I didn't out her secret, but I did ask if he'd ever be able to see her as more than a friend. He looked at me like I'd lost my mind. He told me about their drunken spin the bottle kiss. He said she was the best kiss he'd ever had, and that fact freaked him out more than he thought it would. He thought a kiss from her would be like a kiss from any other girl. But he saw fireworks he wasn't prepared for. His exact words were: *I wanted nothing more than to throw her down right there on that dirty basement floor and fuck her until I couldn't move another muscle.* When I asked him why he'd never act on those feelings, he said: *Because I'd fuck it up and I know I wouldn't survive losing her.*

That was years ago, though, and I don't know if he still feels that way. It's clear how she feels. I can see her love for him every time I look at her. I don't love her the way Preston does. Their love grew from years of close friendship. My love for her started when she came to me the night of her senior prom. I'd finished up my classes early and decided to come home.

The two of them had agreed to go to prom together instead of with dates—one last memory to share before they separated for college. I could tell she was hoping it would finally be the night she got what she'd always wanted. She obsessed over everything. She wore a blue dress because that was his favorite color. She got her hair highlighted because he once said how beautiful her hair was after a summer's worth of sun. She wanted to be perfect for him. She wanted him to see her for the first time—not the version of her he saw every day, but the her she *could* be . . . for him.

But I knew how everything would go down, and I was right. Piper ended up leaving the afterparty the moment Preston locked himself in a room with his ex. I was sitting out by the pool when she found me. Her makeup was smeared from crying and her hair was a mess— once the party was over for her, she'd started taking the pins out of her hair on the limo ride home. She looked sad, lost, broken.

The gate on the privacy fence opens and I turn my attention to it, wondering if Preston left his party early. It's unlikely, but who else could it be? My eyes lock on Piper. She looks like she's been crying, and immediately, my emotions go on high alert. Did Preston cause this? Did he hurt her? I'll fucking kill him if he hurt her.

"Calvin." She says my name and the tears start to fall.

I hold up my arm and motion for her to join me on the patio bench. She races to me, hiding her face in the crook of my neck.

"What's wrong, Pipes? Did something happen?" I ask, hugging her tightly to my side.

She pulls back and wipes the tears from her eyes. "Preston is hooking up with Hannah as we speak, and I mean, I knew there was a possibility he would turn me down, but I didn't expect him to run off with her before I even had the chance to tell him how I feel." She takes a deep breath and lets it out slowly. "Why doesn't he love me, Calvin?" Another tear falls from her eye and rolls down her cheeks.

I reach up and gently wipe the tear away. I've talked to her about my brother many times over the years. "He does love you, Piper. He just doesn't love you the way you want him to."

She nods. It's something I've told her more times than I can count. "What's wrong with me? I mean, am I ugly or something? Please don't lie to make me feel better. Just tell me the truth."

I take a deep breath, slowly releasing it as I lock my eyes on hers. "You're not ugly, Piper. You're beautiful—too beautiful and too good to be with someone like my brother. You see how he is with girls. You really want to be another one of them?"

She rolls her eyes. "At this point, I'll take anything I can get," she says around a giggle. "I guess I was just hoping he'd be different with me. Like yeah, he screws around with a lot of girls, but I thought maybe I could be the one who changes him. The one who makes him see that one girl who loves you is better than 20 who only want you for something. I know it's stupid. He's never going to change."

"I wish I could make this feeling go away for you. I'd take away all your pain if I could, but I can't. This is something you have to take control of yourself. Maybe going off to separate colleges will be the turning point. You know: gain some distance, meet new people, live different lives."

She nods as her eyes slowly move up to lock on mine. With her facing me, our noses are almost touching. She wets her lips and I can't help the overwhelming feeling that consumes me. I want to taste her. I want to feel how soft those lips are—taste their sweetness.

"You're really something special, Pipes. Don't think you're not just because Preston doesn't see what the rest of us do."

Without warning, I close the distance between us. My rough, dry lips press against her soft, smooth ones. She sucks in a breath the moment we touch, but she doesn't pull away, and I'm not sure why. Instead of breaking our kiss, her tongue comes out and dances with mine. My body blazes as I deepen the kiss. My hands cup her cheeks and hers move up to wrap around my neck. She pulls me closer and I feel myself come alive. Just as I'm about to pull her on top of me, I hear the slamming of a car door, and Preston yelling, "Piper! Where are you?"

We quickly pull away just as the back gate opens and he rushes in. "There you are. Why did you leave? Why didn't you tell me? I would've left with you," he says, walking over. She stands up and looks at him, then down at me, and back.

In this moment, I know what she's doing. She's choosing. And she chooses him the moment she takes his hand and lets him walk her away from me.

"Drink that shot!" Piper tells Preston as she pushes the shot glass over to him, pulling me from my memory.

"Seriously? Another one?" he whines.

She smiles and her glassy green eyes light up. "Oh yeah. You've gotten me drunk all weekend. It's your turn. Plus, you have to." She holds up a shot glass of her own and waits until Preston picks up his. They knock the shot glasses together then throw back the liquid.

While they chug another pitcher of beer and chase it with random shots of every kind of alcohol known to man, I sit back and sip my glass of scotch. Piper said only old men drink scotch and that I need to live a little, but I know I won't be the one with my head in the toilet in the morning, so I'll stick with what I know.

"What should we play first? Darts or shuffleboard?" Piper asks, looking between my brother and me.

"Well, I'm out on shuffleboard," I say, showing her my palms.

"All right, darts it is. Plus, all three of us can play darts and I can work on getting Preston a little more drunk so I'll win at shuffleboard too." She gives him an ornery smile as she stands to put some money in the electronic dartboard. "I'm gotta get some change. I'll be right back." She heads toward the bar.

I place my arms on the table and lean in. "So, you two seem just as friendly as ever."

He offers up a smile and nods. "Why wouldn't we be? I'm not the one who ran off to St. Louis for three years."

I shake my head. "What's that got to do with anything?"

"You're jealous of our friendship. You always have been."

I laugh and rub my hands over my face. "What? I am not. I'm just confused is all."

"Confused about what?" His dark brows pull together.

"Last I checked, she was completely in love with you, and you were desperately trying to avoid breaking her heart and having to tell her you don't love her the way she wants. Is that still the case?"

He lets out a long breath that causes his cheeks to balloon out. "Pretty much." He leans in and talks softly so no one overhears. "I love her to death, Calvin. You know that. I just . . . I don't—no, *can't*— I can't see her as anything other than my best friend. I tried. Today we went to the beach and hung out, and as much as I wanted to see if we could work, I couldn't. All I see when I look at her is my best friend. Is she beautiful? Yes. Is she hot? Hell yeah. But would I ever touch her?" He shakes his head as he leans back.

That's all I needed to know. He doesn't love her in that way. He's not going to try to make anything work between them. That's the permission I needed to not feel bad about checking her out

"All right, got the darts and the board is ready. Calvin, you get the red ones." She hands me three red darts. "Preston, you get blue because you're stupid and think that's your lucky color." She hands them over with a breathtaking smile. "And I'm yellow because I'm bright and cheery." Her smile beams.

Preston snorts but stands up and gets himself in front of the board. He pulls his arm back and sends the dart flying, but it misses the board completely. Piper giggles and slides into the booth across the table from me.

"So, what's been going on in your life, Cal? Any new women I need to hear about?"

I laugh and pick up my glass, taking a sip. "Nope, still just as single as always."

"What's the holdup?"

I shrug. "I'm just waiting for the right girl to notice me," I say, hoping I haven't given away too much, but she's been drinking and it flies right over her head. I'm not sure if I'm glad or disappointed.

"Well, I bet she'll find you soon and then wonder how she's overlooked you for so long." She offers up a smile but it quickly falls away when Preston is back at the table. She grabs her darts and stands to throw.

We all take turns throwing darts between taking sips of our drinks. I sit back and laugh when Piper makes Preston get up and embarrass himself by dancing stupidly on the dance floor, singing karaoke, and giving random women his phone number. And it's only women he would have zero interest in.

"Thanks a lot. Now I'm going to have to change my phone number," he complains as he sits down and she hands him another shot. He cocks his head to the side. "Are you trying to give me alcohol poisoning again?"

She lets out an adorable giggle like she has no idea what he's talking about. "To be fair, I didn't give it to you the first time. I told you not to drink that homemade shit those guys were giving you on the beach. I mean, it was literally in a Mason jar. Who in their right mind would drink that?" She looks from him, to me, and back. "I want to dance. Who's volunteering?"

This is my chance, but is now a good time to make a move? I mean, she's drunk and still completely in love with Preston. Even if I did reveal my feelings, she'd probably turn me down.

"Okay, no volunteers, so that means you have to dance with me, Pres. Come on. Let's go." She stands up and takes his hand, pulling him to the dance floor as he groans and pleads.

Almost on cue, the fast, upbeat song turns to a soft, slow one. Instead of walking back to the table, she pulls him against her. I watch as he places his hands softly on her hips. She wraps hers around his neck. He's looking everywhere but at her while her eyes are locked on his face. There's a big smile on her lips. I can't do anything but shake my head and order another glass.

Why does she do this to herself? Doesn't she see that she's only setting herself up for heartbreak? I mean, there's no way he's going to let anything happen between them. Maybe this was her plan all along: get him drunk and see where things lead.

The waitress drops off another glass and I take a sip before looking back over at them. My jaw nearly drops when I see them kissing. It's not a gross, going-at-it kind of kiss. It's a soft, slow kiss it seems they're both enjoying. Anger fills my chest. He just sat here and told me he couldn't ever let anything happen between them, yet he's kissing her?

I want to be mad at both of them, but deep down I can't. I can't be angry with her for kissing him in front of me, because she doesn't know how I feel about her. And I can't be mad at Preston for kissing her, because he has no clue either. They're drunk and being stupid. Who's to say they haven't done this kind of thing before? Maybe that's why she can't get over him. He keeps her dangling—always waiting for him to give her more.

I pretend I don't notice their kiss as I finish off the fresh glass I was just handed. When they make their way back over to the table, I stand up. "I really need to get going. I have to leave early in the morning for a late lunch with a client. Mind taking me home?"

"Yeah, sure," Preston agrees.

Piper doesn't seem happy that I'm ending their drunken time together, but she doesn't say anything as we walk out. When we get to the car, I hold out my hand and Preston gives me the keys. Piper climbs into the back seat and Preston takes the passenger seat. On the way home, I go a different way so we'll pass Piper's house first. That way, I can drop her off before pulling into the drive. That means she won't have to walk across the street to go home . . . and won't have any excuse to stick around with Preston.

I pull up in front of her house and Preston opens his door.

"You didn't have to drop me off, Cal. I could've walked," she says as she tries climbing out.

"It's fine. You're drunk. Didn't want to take the risk of you getting hit by a car while trying to cross the street."

She smiles but holds up a middle finger. I hear her say something to Preston softly, but then she walks to the door. Preston climbs back in and we both watch as she walks to the door and steps inside.

"What was that kiss about?" I ask as I maneuver the car into our driveway across the street.

He holds up his hands and lets them fall into his lap. "I don't know, man. Drunken fun is all."

I park and hand him the keys. "She still kiss as good as she did in high school?"

He rolls his eyes. "Better. If I didn't fear ruining our friendship, I would have gladly left your ass in the bar to screw her in the back seat," he laughs out and I shake my head as I climb out.

I'm heading toward the door when he calls out my name and jogs up behind me. "What's your deal? Why are you acting mad right now? What do you care if we kiss?"

I take a calming breath and pinch the bridge of my nose. "Because, Preston, I'm the one who's had to dry her tears every time you've turned her down for another girl. She's your best friend and she loves you. You keep confusing her like this and you *will* lose her. You either need to step up and be the guy she wants you to be or stop the kissing and innocent flirting so she knows where she stands with you. Either way, I don't care. Just make up your damn mind already!" I turn to walk into the house, but he grabs my shoulder and spins me around.

"I'm sorry if us kissing pissed you off, but the truth is, she's the one girl I'd never let myself have. Excuse me if I can't resist the temptation every once in a while. I mean, could *you*? If she threw herself at you, could you resist, or would you reach out and take her already? Huh? I've seen the way you look at her, Cal. Something tells me you wouldn't be able to resist, either."

Without another word, he walks past me into the house, slamming the door behind him.

SIX
PIPER

My body is tingling and coming alive in ways it never has before. That kiss. I don't even know how it happened. We were dancing, holding each other close. I couldn't take my eyes off him. Suddenly, he looked up and our eyes locked. The next thing I knew, we were kissing. And it was nothing like our last kiss. The last kiss, when we were 16, was amazing—but this kiss was life-changing. Every hair on my body is still standing on end.

When he pulled me back to the table, I thought he was going to insist we go someplace where we could be alone—either to tell me he's always secretly been in love with me or pick up where we left off on the dance floor. But then Calvin wanted to go home, which ruined my evening.

His tone was short and clipped and his face showed no emotion. He didn't look mad, but he didn't look as carefree as before, when we were all playing darts. A part of me wonders if he's jealous, but that's absurd. Calvin and I have never been anything more than friends. Sure, we had one kiss back when I was in high school, but I've always known it didn't mean anything. I was upset and crying, so he kissed me. It was a pity kiss and nothing more.

I'm so confused by Preston and Calvin that I'm nowhere near ready for bed. I'm primed and ready to go; I can't just curl into a ball and drift off to sleep. I go to the kitchen, pour myself a glass of wine, and take it up to my room. I turn on the TV and flip through the channels until I land on some new game show called *Reveal Your Secret*. I toss the remote onto the bed and set my wine on the bedside table as I strip down and slide into my pajamas.

I climb into bed and turn off the light, enjoying my wine while I watch TV. It only takes me a few minutes to catch on to the theme of the show. People have a secret they've kept hidden away from the one they love most, and they bring them on the show to finally reveal it.

I'm watching a woman who's secretly been in love with her best friend's husband for years. She tells her best friend, and as you can imagine, it doesn't go well. As the show continues, I laugh with some, I cry with some, and others are just stupid and pointless. I mean, who cares if you stole a penny candy from the corner market when you were 10? As the credits roll, the announcer gets my attention: "If you have a secret you need to reveal, go to the website at the bottom of your screen. You may just get the chance to reveal your secret!"

Light bulb! I could take Preston to the show. I could finally tell him the secret I've been too afraid to reveal. Wait, let's think this through. Why tell him this secret on the show when you've been too scared to tell him alone? Tonight has definitely changed things, right? I mean, we've never kissed before, other than that stupid game. But tonight we kissed on our own. Maybe that kiss was his way of saying, "Hey stupid, I like you!" Going on this show could be the grand gesture I need to prove to him that I'm serious. And once we're there, I can't back out. There's no chance I'll chicken out this time.

I grab my computer and go to the website that was promoted on the bottom of the screen. Turns out, the show is filming in Chicago. How perfect is that? I quickly fill in the blanks: name, address, birthdate, and then comes the biggest part of all—the secret.

I have been secretly in love with my best friend for as long as I can remember. His name is Preston Young and he's been my best friend since we were five. We did everything together growing up. Preston is fun-loving, sexy, sweet, and of course, a ladies' man. He's dated almost everyone in our small hometown. Everyone but me. I've had to stand in the shadows for years, watching as every other girl got the one thing I couldn't have. I've gone back and forth wondering if telling him this secret is a good idea or not, but something changed tonight that's making me lean toward telling him. We shared a drunken kiss! It seems there's no better time than now. But how will he feel? Will he love me too or will he turn me down? Only time will tell.

I click the *SEND* button and push my laptop to the side. Sleep is starting to pull at me and I want nothing more than to give in—let it take me to a place where Preston and I can be together in every way I want.

———

I WAKE in the morning and the hangover I've been putting off all weekend is making itself known again. I grab the bottle of Tylenol out of my purse and wash two down. I take a quick shower, not worrying about my appearance since I won't be doing anything but driving most of the day. I quickly throw my things into my bag, carry it downstairs, and set it by the door. I head toward the kitchen where I smell coffee and breakfast.

"Good morning. Aren't you looking a little rough?" Mom says with the sweetest smile as I plop down on the barstool at the island. "Coffee?"

"Please," I mumble.

She shakes her head and rolls her eyes, but eventually goes to pour me a cup of coffee. She sets it in front of me with a plate covered in eggs, bacon, toast, and fresh fruit.

"Thank you," I say, wasting no time digging in.

"How was the weekend with Preston?" she asks, loading the dishwasher.

"Good. I'm glad we decided to come home at the same time,

although I feel like I wasted all weekend and didn't get to spend any time with you guys. When are you planning on coming into the city?"

"It's fine, hon. You know your dad. He avoids the city every chance he gets. Plus, we'll be having our big Fourth of July cookout soon. You'll make it back for that, right?"

"Of course. I never miss it. I wait all year for the Independence Day punch." I smile at the memory until the thought of alcohol turns my stomach.

She laughs. "One of these days you'll settle down."

I snort. "Don't hold your breath." I push my plate away now that my stomach has decided it doesn't want food. "I should hit the road before traffic picks up." I stand and kiss the top of her head while she gently hugs me.

"Call me when you get home so I know you got back safe."

"I will. Love you."

"Love you too," she says just as I'm opening the front door and walking out.

I toss my bag into the back seat and open the driver's side door. I glance over at the Youngs' home, hoping to see Preston one more time. I see his car in the driveway, but Calvin is already gone, and neither of them is outside. I climb behind the wheel to start my drive.

With the weekend traffic, it takes me almost twice as long to get home, but I finally arrive and I'm more than excited to spend the day lounging around in silence. I take a long, hot bath in my clawfoot bathtub filled with bubbles and oils. I nearly fall asleep, but I force myself to get out and start some laundry for the workweek. I pull on my silky robe and throw all my clothes from my bag into the washer. Once it's started, I pop a bag of popcorn and grab some water to take to the couch.

I start a movie, and while the trailers play, I decide to check my email in case work sent me something over the weekend. The first message in my inbox is from *Reveal Your Secret*.

What's that?

Confused, I click on the email.

Congratulations! You've been chosen to come on our show to reveal your secret! Please respond within 24 hours to set up your taping date.

What the fuck did I do? I scroll down to where it shows what I sent them. I read over the short paragraph. No! No, no, no, no, no! Why did I do that? Why can't I remember it? Screw the why. I *know* why. I was drunk and high off that kiss. *That kiss.* Holy shit, I nearly forgot about that kiss! Shit. Shit, shit, fuck, damn, shit. Twenty-four hours? I have a day to decide. Clearly, I have to pass on this. I mean, Preston is not in love with me.

Or is he?

I can't decide, so I call Riley, my best friend from work.

"'Sup, bitch? How was your weekend?" She sounds happy and cheerful.

"I fucked up, Riley. I mean, I really fucked up."

She giggles. "Let's hear it."

I tell her all about my weekend with Preston since she already knows about my crush. Then I tell her about the kiss and how I drunkenly sent that email to the show and how they've somehow decided I'd be a great guest. "What do I do now?"

"Duh, go on the show!"

"Seriously? You really think now is the time to tell him how I feel?"

"Why not? I mean, you guys *did* kiss. Maybe he feels the same as you but he's afraid to say it because he's scared of what it will change between you two."

"I know, I thought of that too. But what if he doesn't feel the same way? It will crush me. Do I really need that televised?"

She laughs. "Probably not, but I bet you'd end up with a date or two out of it. Guys would see that show and be like, 'Hey, she's hot and I'm in Chicago. Let's look up!'"

"I don't know, Riley. This isn't just some joke. This is my life—and Preston's life—we're talking about."

"Duh, but at least this way you can't back out. We both know if you called him right now with the intention of telling him, you'd back out at the last second. Come on, Piper. *Do it.* You've never been a chicken before. Just take that step! Put this to bed already."

I take a long breath. She's right. It's like a Band-Aid. I just need to rip it off and put it out there. If he doesn't feel the same, fine. I'll get over it and move on. But if he does, I'll finally have everything I've ever wanted.

"Okay, I'm going to do it!"

She squeals with excitement.

I hang up the phone and get back to the email, confirming I'd love to be on their show when I reveal my secret. Now that it's set and done, the nerves kick in. I wonder how long it will take. Now that I'm ready to tell him my secret, I'm not sure how long I can wait. I keep telling myself I've waited all these years, so a few more weeks won't hurt.

I don't get an email from them until the next day, when I check my personal email while I'm on my lunch break. It's only one week away. I can wait seven days. I've given them even more information about Preston—his home address, email, and place of work. They'll take all the necessary steps to get him to come to the set without telling him why he's actually there.

———

THE NEXT WEEK passes at an unbearably slow speed. But it's finally the big day. Preston believes he's going on the show to talk about his job. He's all kinds of excited. He thinks the topic of the show is "jobs you never knew you wanted." Not many people know about his job, and he's looking forward to reaching kids who aren't settled on a career. He thinks he can get the job in the mainstream.

I made it very clear that I would be going with him for support. We drive to the studio together and he's immediately taken to a private dressing room. Normally, I'd stick right by his side, but keeping this secret now that it's on the tip of my tongue is getting harder and harder. It seems to take forever, but I'm finally ushered to the stage. The set lights are hot, and unfortunately for me, this is a live taping, which means the audience is full of inquisitive eyes. I try to look cool and collected, but I feel awkward and embarrassed. Right now would be a great time to run.

"So, Piper, tell us a little about your secret," Jefrey, the host, says from his nice, comfy chair.

I swallow down my fear and wet my lips before looking at the camera. "I've known my best friend, Preston, since we were five. We've been the best of friends and have done everything together."

"And why have you brought Preston here? What do you want to say to him?"

I chew on my inner cheek as I think over my words. "I've brought Preston here to tell him I'm secretly in love with him."

The crowd gasps dramatically and I can feel my face heating up.

Jefrey looks at the camera. "Preston is backstage right now. He thinks he's here to talk about his job. After the break, we'll tell him why he's *really* here. We'll be right back."

The red light on the camera turns off and I feel myself relax. Suddenly, my mind starts racing. Maybe this wasn't a good idea. If I change my mind, I wonder if they'll bring Preston out here to talk about his job—you know, to keep the lie going and keep me out of trouble. I doubt it. Can I do this? In front of everyone?

I expected the commercial break to last . . . I don't know, as long as a commercial break usually does when you watch TV, but that isn't the case. Before I know it, they're counting us down and mouthing *Action!* Jefrey stands up. "Everyone, please give a warm welcome to Preston." He gestures to the side of the stage.

Preston walks to the stage and the women in the audience go wild. He smiles and even blushes a bit as he waves at them on his walk over. Then he shakes Jefrey's hand and sits down. He looks over and finds me. His brows pull together slightly. He's confused as to why I'm onstage with him. I was only supposed to be here for support.

"Preston, do you know this woman?" Jefrey asks him.

Preston looks from Jefrey, to me, and back. "Yes, this is my best friend, Piper."

Jefrey nods and smiles. "That's right. And how long have the two of you been friends?"

Preston sits up straight as he looks at me. His body is hard while his back stays completely rigid. "Since we were five. What is this about?"

"Well, Preston, you're not really here to talk about your job."

"I'm not?" His brows shoot up as his eyes widen.

"No, you're here because Piper has something to tell you. Don't you, Piper?"

I feel everyone's eyes on me and my skin's so hot, I expect flames to erupt. "I do," I agree, sitting a little taller. I offer him a smile as I reach over and take his hand in mine. "I brought you here today because I have a secret to tell you," I confess.

His face falls. He's worried.

"After that drunken kiss we had the other night, I thought now would be a good time to tell you something I've never been able to tell you." I swallow down my fear. "Preston, I love you. I've been in love with you for as long as I can remember."

His mouth drops open and his eyes take in the audience in front of us. "You . . . what?" he asks around a nervous laugh.

I nod. "I know this must be a surprise. I mean, we're friends and that's all we've ever been. We've never crossed the line . . . well, until the other night. That's why I thought maybe you felt the same way and were just too afraid to say it."

He shakes his head clear but his face reddens and he sets his jaw. "Why? Why did you bring me here? I can't." He stands up and starts pulling off his mic. "I'm sorry, I can't do this. Not here. Not like this." The crowd gasps as Preston makes his way off the stage.

I look from Jefrey, to the crowd, and then to the side where

Preston just left the stage. My body feels heavy, like I have sandbags tied to my ankles. My heart feels weary. What did I just do? He hates me. I want to get up and chase after him—explain my side of things and tell him I'm sorry for embarrassing him. What if he leaves? What if this is the last chance I get?

Without thinking, I find the strength to jump up and chase after him. I run backstage and find him exiting the dressing room. He has his hat and jacket in his hands. He's really leaving.

"Preston, wait!" I shout as I run to catch up with him.

He spins around to face me, and I've never in my life seen this look directed at me—his parents, his brother, or somebody at school, sure. But never me.

"I'm sorry," I breathe out.

He shakes his head. "What were you thinking, Piper? Did you honestly think doing it this way would work out for you? Huh? Did you think, 'Hey, maybe he'll just go along with it to keep from embarrassing me'?"

"No, I just wanted to make a grand gesture, Preston. This secret was big and I wanted you to see—"

"Your *secret*," he says, using air quotes, "wasn't that big of a secret, Piper! I've known for years."

"You have?" I ask, finding myself rethinking every moment we've spent together over the years. "Then why didn't you say anything?"

"Because I didn't want to hurt you." He shakes his head and rubs his temples. "I've gotta get out of here."

"But I rode with you," I point out as he turns to leave.

He stops dead in his tracks, turns around, and pulls out his wallet. "Here, get a taxi. I just . . . need to be alone right now." He stuffs the cash into my hand. "I'm sorry, Pipes. I just can't." Without another word, he turns and leaves.

It's only now I notice the host and the cameraman standing behind me. They recorded everything. Tears threaten to fall as embarrassment washes over me.

"And *cut*," someone yells, just as a production assistant rushes over to me with a clipboard in her hands.

"That was great stuff, Piper. Here's your copy of the release form." She hands over the paper like it's a reminder I already signed it and can't stop this from getting out. "Your air date will be announced. Thanks for coming in." Everyone walks away, leaving me standing alone.

SEVEN

PIPER

I t's a Saturday night and it's been two weeks since the taping. Tonight is the night my embarrassment airs for the world—or at least the United States—to see. Still, it's more people watching my rejection than I want. I haven't talked to Preston since the day he left me standing in the studio alone. I've wanted to call him so many times over the last couple weeks, but something's always stopped me. I'm deathly afraid he'll call off our friendship. I mean, I couldn't blame him. I did embarrass him on national TV. But I also keep telling myself to give him some time. Let him calm down so maybe he can see past his embarrassment and anger.

Riley has promised to watch the show and tell me how bad it is. I can't bring myself to watch it. I'm still living it every day—every time I close my eyes. I don't need to see it played out on my 32-inch TV screen in high-def. The only thing I'm happy about is that the show doesn't air until 11 p.m. How many people are going to watch a low-rated, late-night show on basic cable on a Saturday night? People have lives, you know.

All evening, I've been preparing myself for the airing by emptying a bottle of wine. Around 11, I fill the bathtub, adding in my favorite oils and bubbles. I light candles and spread them around the room as I dim the lights. I sink into the tub with my glass of wine and listen as soft music plays.

I finish my glass and am feeling relaxed when my cell rings. That's when all the stress returns. Riley promised to call after the show to discuss my chances of recovering from the embarrassment.

I tap the screen to answer the call and put it on speaker. "Well?" I ask.

"Ouch," she says,

I groan. "That bad?"

"The camera followed the two of you off stage. It was like an episode of *Springer!*"

I fake a crying sound. "It felt like I was on an episode of *Springer.*"

"Honestly, though, I don't think it made you look bad. I mean, you were there looking all cute and innocent and hopeful. Then there was Preston. He just looked like a jerk. I mean, he drove you there and left you! If I were you, I wouldn't feel bad for myself. And I don't think the rest of the country is looking at you the way you think. Preston on the other hand . . ."

"Well, that's not good either, Riley. He's the last person I wanted to be hurt. He's my best friend and I embarrassed him."

"Have you talked to him yet?"

"No. It's been two weeks! We've never gone this long without talking. I really screwed up. I miss my best friend."

"Maybe you should call him," she suggests.

"No way! Not after that. Not when I made the whole country look at him like he's the bad guy!"

"Okay. But soon. Promise me you won't let this tear you two apart."

I take a deep breath. "When the time is right, I will call," I promise.

"Good. Now I have a date. Call if you need anything."

"You have a midnight date?"

"Yes, that cutie I was telling you about asked me out, but I'd already promised to watch the show and I couldn't let you down."

I smile. "I love you, you know."

I can practically hear the smile in her tone. "I know."

The phone gets disconnected and I drain the tub to go for more wine. I dry off and wrap my silk robe around my body as I walk to the kitchen. I set my wine glass on the counter and open the fridge. There's a dinging sound I've never heard the fridge make before.

Confused, I close the door and open it again to see if it makes the same sound. It doesn't. I shrug my shoulders and grab the bottle of wine. Just as I'm uncorking it, I hear the sound again, this time realizing it's the doorbell.

What the fuck is wrong with me?

I open the front door that hardly ever gets used since I always go out the garage door. I'm surprised to find Calvin standing on the other side. He's dressed in a perfectly-tailored suit. His hair is styled nicely and he's holding a bouquet of flowers and a bottle of wine.

The moment I see him, I know. He's seen the show.

"Come to bandage the wounds?" I ask, reaching out and taking the bottle of wine. I turn and leave him at the door as I work on opening the bottle.

He walks in and closes the door behind him. "It wasn't that bad," he says, laying the flowers on the coffee table in the living room. I uncork the bottle and take a gulp.

"Wasn't that bad? You did see the correct show, right? The one where I confessed my love for your bother and got my heart broken?" I take the bottle to the living room and plop onto the couch.

He takes the seat next to me. When he does, his deep, rich scent settles over me. Somehow, I find the smell relaxing—calming. I tip up the bottle and take a long drink before resting my head on his shoulder like always.

"How many times are we going to be here?" I ask, mostly thinking out loud.

"This is the first time I've ever been to your place. It's nice. I like it."

I laugh. "No, I meant . . . *here.* Me crying and heartbroken over your stupid brother and you giving me a shoulder to cry on. Aren't you sick of doing this for me? I'm stupid for still being caught up in him."

He takes a deep breath and reaches for the bottle. "The show wasn't bad, Piper. If anything, it just made Preston look like the dick he can sometimes be. He shouldn't have kissed you. You deserve someone who can love you back."

"I know. And while I do love Preston, it's becoming clear it never should've gone as far as it did. He's my best friend and I don't want to lose him. I just hope he forgives me."

"He will," he promises.

"How do you know?"

"Do you know why Preston doesn't want to be with you?"

"He doesn't want to ruin our friendship." I state the same thing I've been told time and time again.

"Yes, but that's not all of it. Preston loves you. You're his best friend. And I think a part of him does want you in the way you wish he would. You're beautiful and fun to be around. Any man who's not attracted to you is stupid. Preston wants you to be another one of his girls, but he knows that could never happen. He isn't ready to change. He isn't looking for a relationship. All he's looking for is a good time. He knows he can't get away with treating you the way he treats the rest of them. I mean, even if things went great at the beginning, you'd eventually want more, and he's not willing to give it to anyone. That would cause you to leave him. He needs you so much more than you know. So to him, it's either have you as his best friend—the person he runs to with every bit of good news, and the person who's always there to pick him up when he's down—or take what he wants to take but then not have anyone to run to. I love my brother to death, but he sometimes uses people to feel better about himself. He doesn't want to hurt you. In my eyes, this is the best thing he's ever done for you. Now you know where you stand and you can finally move on."

I lift my head off his shoulder and take the bottle of wine back, enjoying another sip. "What if I don't find anyone else? What if no one wants to be with me?"

He reaches out and takes away the bottle of wine, setting it on the coffee table in front of us as he turns to look me in the eyes. "That's never going to happen. You're beautiful, Piper. You're a good person. Any guy would be lucky to have you."

"How am I ever going to get over this embarrassment though? I was abandoned on public television, Calvin!"

He chuckles. "No one's watching that shit, Piper. I only watched it because Preston told me about it the day it happened. Though I had to do some digging to find out when your episode would air since Preston acted like he couldn't remember."

"You really don't think it was that bad? Or are you just trying to make me feel better?"

He smiles and it causes his dimples to show. "Both," he answers. His icy eyes light up and it feels like they're cutting straight into my soul. Why haven't I ever seen Calvin in this way before? He's good-looking—drop-dead sexy if I'm being honest. He's mature—outshining Preston in every way. Sure, Preston is fun, but that's because he's still a child in so many ways. Calvin has always seemed to know when I needed a shoulder to cry on, whereas Preston never noticed because he was off having too much fun.

"Thank you, Calvin. For everything. For all the years of talking sense into me, for making me feel better about myself, and everything in between. Growing up, I don't know what I would've done if I hadn't had you in my life."

His smile stays in place as his hand lands on my knee, gently squeezing. "No problem, Pipes. And don't worry about Pres. He'll come around."

"So, you wanna sit and get drunk with me? Some guy brought me a bottle of pity wine, and this isn't my first bottle of the night." I reach forward and grab the bottle he set down, taking a sip with a smile before handing it over.

"Don't mind if I do." He takes the bottle and looks at the label. "Hey, this is good stuff, too. That guy must have good taste." With a smile of his own, he takes a drink.

We take turns passing the bottle of wine back and forth while talking about the show. Somehow, Calvin makes me see certain things I didn't notice before. We make fun of the crowd's dramatic reactions. By their gasps, you would've thought I admitting to killing his dog or something. We make fun of cheesy Jefrey. Calvin says he thinks he saw him in an old '80s porno, and I lose it. I'm laughing so hard I can't catch my breath. I laugh until I somehow manage to fall off the couch and onto my ass, which only makes both of us laugh harder.

While laughing, Calvin holds out his hand to help me up. I grab ahold of it, but instead of pulling against him to get up, I pull him down with me. It's fair to say the good wine did its job. We're both tipsy and in the giggly phase.

Calvin lands on his hip, which has somehow managed to wedge between my hip and the couch. He's lingering halfway over me. He has one hand on the floor beside my head. As our laughing settles down, he looks into my eyes and something is exchanged. I wet my lips and lift my head until they're pressed against his.

I don't even know why I'm kissing him. All I know is that it feels good. His lips are soft but strong as they slowly start to move against mine. His tongue is sweet, tasting like the wine we've been drinking, and his hard body, which is pressed against mine, causes my skin to burn with excitement.

It's only now I realize I'm only wearing my silk robe. I'm completely naked beneath it, and it would take nothing to push it away and reveal myself to him. I should be worried, but this only excites me more. I wrap my arms around his neck and pull him closer. He kisses me back softly and slowly until I nip his lower lip. When I do that, it's like I threw gasoline on a fire. Something inside him changes and the kiss picks up intensity. Instead of staying at my side, I find him on top of me, his hips between my parted thighs. I feel him harden against my core and I can't help the soft whimper that escapes. I reach for his belt buckle, but the moment my fingers wrap around it, he breaks the kiss and pulls away. He stands up, pulling me up with him.

"I'm sorry, Piper. I should go." Without another word, his back is turned and he's heading for the door. Hearing it close feels like a bucket of ice water being dumped over my head.

I fall back onto the couch with tears in my eyes. What's wrong with me? Why do I do this shit? I'm sure Calvin is just thinking, *Since she can't have Preston, she wants me as a last resort.* That's not the case at all, even though I can see why he might think that.

Maybe I should've listened to that tingle in my belly instead of still chasing after Preston the night Calvin and I first kissed. None of this would've happened. Truth is, I never should've blurred the lines with Preston in the first place. I should've seen Calvin back then. I should've seen how good he was—how mature he was compared to the guys I was dating. I should've seen that he was always the one who was there for me.

Now I have this huge mess on my hands and I have no idea how to fix it.

EIGHT

CALVIN

I never should've gone over there. I should've known I'd end up doing something stupid. But *fuck*, kissing her felt good. Too good. I don't know how I managed to pull myself away from her, but I'm glad I did it. She was drunk and upset and still beating herself up over my brother. Getting together with her now wouldn't have been good for anyone. Deep down, I wonder if I'm just the closest thing she can get to Preston, and that's the only reason she kissed me. That's not how I want things to get started with us.

When we come together—*if* we come together—I want it to be for the right reasons. Not because she's hurting or drunk or just trying to get over some other guy. I want her to choose me for me. I want her to want me as much as I want her.

I only went over there because that's what I do. In the past, every time something happened with my brother, I was the one she ran to. I knew she wouldn't come running this time. I did what I thought I needed to do. It's now easy to see that it was just another mistake.

When I get home, I'm surprised to see Preston's car in the parking lot. I park and get out, walking into the building and riding the elevator up to my penthouse suite. He's trying to get on the elevator as I'm trying to get off.

"Hey, what brings you here so late at night?" I ask, stepping into the hallway and leading him to my door, where I take out my keys to unlock it.

"The show aired tonight."

"I know. I watched it."

He lets out a heavy sigh. "And? How big of an asshole was I?"

I open the door and let us both in. "A pretty big asshole," I agree. "Why did you react that way? She's your best friend."

He runs his hands through his dark hair. "I know. I was just surprised that she chose to tell me on a TV show. It pissed me off. I mean, why couldn't she just tell me without an audience?" He plops down on the couch and I grab us two bottles of beer.

I hand one over and sit in the chair beside him. I laugh and wipe my hand down my face. "I don't know. It's Piper. She's not exactly known for her rational thinking, you know. She was just confused. I told you that would happen after you kissed."

"It was just a drunken kiss. I didn't know she'd read so much into it."

"Have you talked to her?"

He shakes his head. "Not since I left her on set."

"Don't you think you should? I mean, she's embarrassed and worried you'll never speak to her again."

"How do you know that?" he asks, pulling his brows together.

"I was just over there. Figured she'd need a friend after the airing. I took her some flowers and a bottle of wine."

He lets out a long breath. "Why didn't I think of that? What did she say?"

My eyes are wide when I say, "Like I said before, she's embarrassed and afraid you'll never speak to her again!"

"I meant after you talked her down." He takes a sip.

"Well . . ." I start, but I have no idea how to tell him. I refuse to hide it. He should know. "We sort of got drunk and maybe kissed."

"What?" he asks, eyes wide with surprise as he springs to his feet. "How the hell did that happen?"

I shrug. "You know Piper. She got drunk and we were talking and laughing and having a good time. It just sort of happened, but I stopped it immediately and left."

He falls back on the couch, shaking his head and groaning. "Guess I'm not the only Young to kiss Pipes."

Confession time. "Actually, Preston . . . that wasn't the first time we'd kissed."

His eyes leap up to mine. "What? When?"

"Years ago. On your prom night. She arrived at our home upset because she was planning on telling you how she felt about you at prom, but then you left her to go into a room with your ex. She came over and cried on my shoulder. We ended up kissing that night."

"I remember that night. I walked in the back gate and the two of you were sitting next to each other."

I nod. "Yeah, you sort of interrupted us."

"I had no idea. I was just so worried I upset her that I had to find her and fix everything."

"You did upset her, but like always, I was there to calm her down."

"So what? You have, like, a thing for her now?"

I shrug, not really wanting to admit anything. "I don't know. I mean, I've always kind of been attracted to her. It's just that she was so young and I had so much going on with school. And she was completely in love with you, so I didn't want to make a move. Now I've *made* a move and I'm afraid she only kissed me because I'm the closest thing to you."

"So you kissed her first?"

I shake my head. "No, she kissed me, but I kissed her back."

"Well, you have my permission to see where things lead if that's why you're telling me."

I nod, not sure if that's even why I'm telling him. "I don't know. I think she needs time to heal from all of this. Time to get over you and see what it is she really wants in a relationship."

"Yeah, I am pretty hard to get over," he jokes, giving me a smirk.

I roll my eyes. "You need to go to her. Talk to her and hear her out. Stop being a dick about it all."

"I know," he agrees. "I will. Just not tonight. We both need time to clear our heads."

"Well, you're more than welcome to crash here if you want."

"Nah, I'm going to head back home. Try to sleep it off. Today has been shitty and I bet tomorrow won't be any better. I've already received so many calls, texts, and social media messages about the show that I had to turn off my phone."

"I can't believe people actually watch that shit. Don't people have lives?" I laugh.

"You watched it!" he points out.

"Yeah, but only because of you two dumbasses!"

He waves off my comment and stands, setting his empty bottle on the table. "I'll talk to you later, man."

I offer a wave as I bring my own bottle to my lips.

He turns. "I'm serious. If you like her—like, *really* like her—then go for it. She deserves a good guy like you. But you'd better treat her right. Don't be stupid like me."

"Thanks, man." I sit back and watch him leave, getting up to lock the door behind him.

Now that I'm alone, I can't do anything but think of every moment I've shared with her. I see us playing football in the open field behind my parents' house. I see all the Halloweens we went trick-or-treating together. I see us growing up. I wonder if she's ever looked at me the way she looks at Preston. I wonder if she'll ever be able to look at me that way.

I push all thoughts from my mind and go for a shower before bed. I easily find sleep, but it's not dreamless. Behind my lids, I see memories of her. Even in my sleep, she haunts me.

I GIVE it a few days to let things cool off before I text her.

I'm really sorry about the other night. Forgive me? I hit *SEND* and lay the phone on my desk as I turn back to my work. Truth is, I haven't been able to focus on anything since that night. I haven't been able to do anything but think of her and how good she felt pressed against me.

My phone dings and I quickly pick it up to read what she sent.

I don't know why I expected you to treat me any differently than Preston. You did the exact same thing he did. You kissed me and ran away. I guess it runs in the family, huh?

Anger fills my chest. How could she even compare me with Preston? We're different in every way possible. I start typing.

Are you serious? You're comparing me with him? I left before things could get too serious. Things you may have woken up to regret. I'm not Preston, Piper. I never will be.

I don't bother setting the phone down. I keep it in my hands and my eyes don't leave the screen as I wait for her reply. I watch as the bubbles dance while she types.

You ever think maybe I kissed you because I like that you're not Preston? That I realized you're the one who has always been there for me? I didn't kiss you because I was drunk or because Preston turned me down. I kissed you because I wanted to kiss you. YOU. Not him. But you ran off just like him, leaving me feeling even more ashamed.

My fingers type quickly. *I didn't ask you to kiss me. I just wanted to check on you and make sure you were okay. If you're feeling ashamed, that's all on you.*

Okay, maybe I shouldn't have sent that, but fuck, she can get me angry like no one else. She kisses me then blames me for feeling ashamed . . . and all because I felt it was bad timing? Doesn't she see that I've always been there for a reason? I'm nothing like my brother. Comparing me with him only angers me.

I push away from my desk and leave the office for the day. I leave everything behind but my phone and keys, knowing I'm too strung up to do anything else. Instead of getting in the car and driving home to marinate in my anger, I walk outside and breathe in the fresh air. I inhale deeply, letting it calm me and take away my frustration.

I walk for at least an hour before I sit on a park bench and type out another message.

I'm sorry. I shouldn't have said that. Take a walk with me. Let's start over.

I wait and wait for a reply but nothing comes in. Just as I'm about to give up, my phone dings.

Where are you?

I smile as I send her my location.

Okay, be there in 20.

I can't force the smile off my face as I sit on the bench and watch everyone walking and riding bikes around me. It feels like no time has passed when a cab stops in front of me and she climbs out. The wind blows her long skirt around her. Her blonde hair is curled like always, hanging halfway down her back, and she's wearing a white T-shirt with a jean jacket over it.

She comes to sit at my side and neither of us talks for a moment as we try to figure out what it is we need to say.

"I'm sorry for letting things get out of hand last night. I'm not sorry about the kiss, but I'm sorry it happened when we were drunk and you were hurting," I finally manage to get out.

She offers up a weak smile and nods her head. "I'm sorry about what I texted you. It's not you. You were great. I just . . . I keep fucking up. I knew Preston didn't feel that way about me and I tricked myself into believing a drunken kiss was his way of telling me he had feelings for me. I went about telling him in the wrong way, and worst of all, I realized you've been in front of me my whole life and I've done nothing but take advantage of your kindness. Can we start over?"

"Clean slate?" I ask, wondering if this is really what we need to get us to where we need to be.

She nods. "You're too good a friend to lose, Calvin. Especially over something like this."

I take her hand in mine and offer her a smile. "Deal."

She lets out a long, drawn-out breath. "Good. Now, how about some ice cream while we walk?"

I laugh. "Whatever you want," I agree.

We get up and walk across the street, going into the ice cream shop. As we stand in line waiting to order, I can't help but watch her as she reads over the sign detailing the flavors. Just thinking about ice cream has her smiling. Her eyes are lit up and her skin is practically glowing. She's fucking breathtaking and I don't get how my brother doesn't see it. He's a fucking idiot as far as I'm concerned.

We step up and order our ice cream. I get one scoop of vanilla on a sugar cone and she orders two scoops of mint chocolate chip. When they're handed over, her eyes stretch wide with excitement. I hand over some cash to pay, but I can't keep my eyes off her as she licks the ice cream. I hate to admit it, but it makes my jeans a little tighter.

We continue on our walk and find ourselves in the park, sitting on a bench and watching the ducks splash around in the water. She's working double time to eat her ice cream before it melts all over her hand. I laugh and she glances at me from the side of her eye.

"What are you laughing at?"

"You trying to eat it before it melts. That's why I only got one scoop." I bite into my cone.

She rolls her eyes. "I didn't think about it," she admits, licking the melted ice cream off her finger as it runs over the side of the cone.

"Give me that," I say, reaching over and taking her cone. I knock the top of it onto my cone and hand it back.

"Hey, you stole my ice cream!" She frowns in the cutest way possible.

I laugh. "It's better than it melting all over you and making you sticky, isn't it?"

She shrugs. "I do hate being sticky." She goes back to licking.

"So, are you going to pursue an acting career now that you've had your first 15 minutes of fame?" I jokingly ask.

She snorts. "No way. I've already had enough eyes on me. I don't need more."

"You looked good on there though," I blurt out.

She laughs. "Yeah, real good getting rejected." She rolls her eyes and her cheeks turn a slight shade of pink from reliving the embarrassing moment.

"I bet no one even noticed. They saw you and were blindsided."

She shakes her head but the corners of her mouth lift a tad. "I don't know how you do it, Calvin."

"What's that?" I ask, licking the mint ice cream.

"Make me feel better. I mean, my whole life you've been there to pick me up and dust me off. And you've never asked for anything in return. If every guy were like you, this world would be a better place."

I offer her a smile before turning my gaze to the water. I can only hope she takes her observation to heart.

We sit on the bench for a long while, talking and finishing our ice cream. We talk about things going on in our lives, plus our favorite books and movies. I'm blown away when she claims to have never seen *Fight Club* and I insist that she watch it.

"I'll find it and we'll have a movie night. Deal?"

She laughs and nods. "Deal," she agrees.

It's going on 8 p.m. by the time I put her in a taxi and close the door. I step back and watch as she gets farther and farther away. When she's no longer in view, I head back to the office to get my car so I can drive home. I know I have a copy of *Fight Club* somewhere and I'm going to find it.

When I make it home, I open up the cabinet that holds my DVDs, CDs, and Blu-ray discs. This cabinet doesn't get opened much, because like most people, I watch most movies on demand nowadays. I pull out the DVD with a smile.

I take my phone out of my pocket and call her number, happy to tell her I found the movie. I can't think of a better way to spend the evening than watching my favorite movie with her, even though I'll probably watch her more than the movie.

"Hey, what's up?" she answers.

"Good news. I found the movie. Still up for a movie night?"

"Oh. Well, actually, Preston just got here and we have a lot of things to talk about. Rain check?"

"Yeah, sure," I agree, feeling let down and maybe even slightly angry. "I'll talk to ya another time." Without saying goodbye, I hang up the phone. I place the DVD on the table and sink into the couch. I thought today would be a turning point for us. I thought our friendship was growing. Hell, we even flirted a bit. I thought she was starting to see what I've been praying for her to see for years now. But like always, Preston's there to screw things up.

What's he even doing there right now? I know they have a lot to talk about and a lot of air between them that needs to be cleared, but did he have to pick tonight to do it? And what if he's changed his mind? What if he's suddenly realized that Piper is the right person for him to settle down with? What am I going to do if he chooses her? I know she'll choose him. I can't walk around the rest of my life knowing the only girl I've ever loved is with my little brother. I can't lose this chance.

I grab my keys off the table and head for the door. I have to see her. I have to tell her how I feel.

NINE

PIPER

I haven't been home very long when the doorbell rings. I'm surprised when I see Preston standing on the other side. My mouth opens to say something, but no words come out. My body is screaming at me to jump into his arms and hold him tightly—to prevent him from leaving and never speaking to me again. I can live without having Preston as my other half, but I can't live without having him as my best friend. I need him in my life.

"Hey," he says, offering up a small smile.

"Hey," I reply, stepping back and holding the door open for him. "Want to come in?"

He nods and steps forward. I close the door behind him and he takes a seat on the couch. I can't help but feel nervous as I make the journey over to him. He sits on one end of the couch and I sit on the other, wanting to keep my distance.

"You wanted to explain, so explain."

I nod and take a deep breath. "First, let me start by saying how sorry I am for taking you on that stupid show. I know it was a bad idea. I just . . . the night I applied for it was the night we kissed. We kissed on that dance floor and then Calvin wanted to leave right after, and it felt like there was unfinished business between us. I was hoping we'd kissed because you've always secretly felt something for me too."

I risk looking up at him, but he isn't looking at me. He's staring straight ahead, so I continue. "I got home that night and I was drunk, but I wasn't tired. I was fueled by that kiss. I wanted to do so much more and it felt like I was left high and dry. So I got into bed and flipped through the channels and found that show. At the end was a casting call, and in my drunken stupor, I thought it was a good idea. I thought it would be a grand gesture to show you how much you mean to me. The next day, I'd forgotten all about it until I received an email stating I'd been chosen. I went back and forth on going through with it, but I thought that if I did it—actually went on the show—that it would keep me from backing out. I'd decided many times over the years that I was finally going to tell you, but when it came down to it, I'd always chickened out."

My phone rings and I pick it up off the table and answer it. It's Calvin, and as much as I want to watch that movie with him, fixing what I broke with Preston is more important right now. Calvin sounds like he understands, and we agree to do movie night some other time.

"I just . . . I don't understand why you couldn't just tell me. Why embarrass us both on that show?" he asks.

I roll my eyes in an attempt to hold back the tears. "Because I suck. You know this," I laugh out and he laughs with me.

He finally turns to me and takes both of my hands in his. "I love you, Piper. I really do. You're my best friend and the only person other than my brother who has always had my back. And that's exactly why I can't go there with you. God, I wish I fucking *could* go there with you. I see how perfect it could be. I really do. And it's not because I don't find you attractive or anything like that, because you're beautiful and perfect. I just need you in my life every single day. And throwing dating, sex, marriage, and all of that on top of it would kill us. We'd end up hating each other and losing a lifetime of friendship. I can't risk losing you."

I nod as a tear finally wells up and falls down my cheek.

He releases one of my hands and wipes it away. "Every decision I make is to protect us—to protect you and our friendship. I won't ever make a choice that could ruin us, Piper."

I do my best to dry my tears. "I know, Preston, and that's why I love you too. I'll admit, the line got a bit blurred there for me, but this time apart has taught me something: I can live without being with you, but I could never live without you in my life."

He smiles. "Good, because I can't live without you in mine either." He pulls me in for a big hug, and even though I don't get exactly what I want, I get exactly what I need. I get his promise to always be in my life—holding my hand when I need it, and protecting me even when I don't know there's danger coming. Preston may not be my happily ever after, but he will be in my ending.

The two of us sit, talk, and catch up on what's been going on since the last time we saw each other. We watch some TV and eat some popcorn. It's pushing 12:30 a.m. when he finally gets up to leave. I lock the door behind him and turn to clean up our mess before taking a shower. As I'm loading the dishwasher, the doorbell rings and I head for the front door thinking Preston must have forgotten something. I don't bother checking the peephole. I just pull the door open with a smile, happy to have my friend back.

"What did you forget?" I ask, just as my eyes land on Calvin. "Oh, I thought you were Pres. What's up?"

He walks in and I close the door behind him, turning to face him. He shakes his head and looks a little nervous, maybe even sick. "I just wanted to check on you. You said that Preston was here and I wanted to make sure things went well."

I nod. "Oh, yeah. Things went great. I explained myself and why I made the horrible choice I did. He explained his side of things, and we came to an agreement that made us both happy."

He sits on the couch, resting his elbows on his knees and leaning forward. "Care to clue me in?"

I sit beside him. "We agreed to be friends. I think he's right. If we were to get together, we'd break up for sure. I mean, we're the same in a lot of ways, but we're also really different. Staying friends is the only way to ensure we'll always have each other."

"And you're okay with this?"

I nod my head. "I'm okay. That doesn't mean I don't have some work to do on my side of things. I mean, it does kind of feel like I've been broken up with even though that's not the case. I just need a little time to clear my head and get over him. I'm not in any hurry to start anything serious. I just need to be me for a while."

He nods his head as he listens. "So the two of you aren't going to start something up?" His brows are pulled together and his jaw is flexed with tension.

I shake my head. "No, not now, not ever. We mean too much to each other to let that happen. I only wish I would've realized it sooner. And honestly, now that I know it, I feel so stupid for not knowing it before. I mean, what would I do if my best friend became my husband, then things went south? Who would I talk to? I wouldn't have my best friend anymore."

He lets out a long, drawn-out breath and seems to be relieved. He's no longer looking sick or nervous. "Good," he breathes out.

Confusion settles over me. "I don't understand." I look up to study his expression.

His icy eyes are trained on mine. His sharp jaw is tightening like he's trying to hold something back, and his back is straight, muscles flexing. "Piper . . . I . . ." He breathes out as he pinches the bridge of his nose and clamps his eyes shut. "Oh, fuck it."

The next thing I know, his mouth is against mine. His tongue comes out and demands entrance. Every inch of my body has hardened with confusion, but that tingle in my stomach begins to form. His lips are soft and warm, and they feel amazing against my own. I don't know what this is. The other night, it was a drunken kiss that was brought on by feeling safe from realizing he's always been there for me. But here he is again, rushing to my side when he thought I might be hurt.

As my brain realizes something my heart has always known, my body relaxes and I pull him closer as I begin to kiss him back. All this time, I've been blinded by Preston. How could I miss Calvin? Something tells me he refuses to let me overlook him any longer. My arms wrap around his neck and his snake around my waist as he lays me back against the couch. His hips make their way between my legs as he covers my body with his without breaking our kiss.

His weight pressing down on me feels right. His hands touring my body feel even better. As his lips kiss their way down my jaw to my neck, his hands begin pushing my shirt up my stomach. Suddenly, his lips are no longer on my neck. Now they're on my stomach, kissing his way up toward my breasts. I know I should stop this. I don't even know what this is. Does Calvin have feelings for me, or is this just a one-time thing? I don't have an answer, but right now, I don't care. His hands, his mouth, his body—it all feels too good to stop.

I haven't been with a man in over a year, and God, do I miss it. I lose all train of thought when his mouth closes around my nipple. He sucks it into his mouth and makes it tingle with excitement. My stomach muscles tighten with anticipation as a flood of want washes over me.

My nails scratch up and down his back before moving between us to unbutton his dress shirt. My hands are nearly shaking, but I manage to get all the buttons undone before loosening his tie. He quickly pulls away and rips the shirt off his arms and the tie over his head. One second later, his mouth is back on mine as he pulls me against him by my waist.

To my surprise, he picks me up against him. "Where's your bedroom?" he asks against my lips, pressing my back to the wall, waiting for me to direct him.

"Through there," I breathe out, nodding toward the hallway that leads to my room.

He jerks me away from the wall and carries me through the hallway and into my bedroom. His hands are supporting my weight by my ass and his mouth never stops moving with mine as he finds my bed and lays me down. I hear him kick off his shoes before crawling up my body, pushing my shirt up as he does so.

Now that we're both lying down with him on top of me, he pushes my shirt the rest of the way up, breaking our kiss for a moment to pull it over my head. It gets tossed to the side, revealing my bra. His mouth moves down to kiss the swell of my breasts and bury his face between them, pressing hot kisses to the skin while his hands work at the clasp. It pops free and he swiftly pulls it off my arms, causing my breasts to bounce with the rough action.

While his mouth devours my breasts, his hands work to unfasten my pants. I tangle my fingers through the silky strands of his hair, tugging his head back slightly to have his eyes lock with mine. He releases my nipple and moves his mouth back to mine.

"You have no idea how long I've dreamt of this, Piper," he whispers against my lips as his hands push my pants down my legs.

I wish I could say the same, but Calvin has only had this effect on me recently. I'm at a loss for words. Instead of lying and telling him the same, I simply say, "Take me, Calvin. Tonight, I'm all yours."

He lets out a growl as his mouth moves back to mine, kissing me hard and rough and pushing me to need more of him. My hands trail down his back, around to his stomach, and then down to the waistband on his dress pants. I unfasten his belt and work on the button. The metal of his belt buckle clanks in the darkness and the sound makes my skin break out in goosebumps. His tongue is dancing with mine when I push his pants over his hips, then I wrap my hand around his length and . . . *oh my God, he's huge!*

I can honestly say I've never even thought about Calvin's manhood before, but he is by far the largest I've ever personally encountered. I can't help but think back on that time I walked in on

Preston and Hannah going at it in high school. Preston has nothing on Calvin. Suddenly, I'm wondering if this is going to hurt. Out of curiosity, I wrap my right hand around his shaft at the base, and then my left hand above my right. I have both hands on him right now and he's still not completely covered. This man better marry me, because I'm going to be ruined after this.

Even with both of my hands wrapped around him, I'm amazed to find that my middle finger doesn't touch my thumb on the other side of him. Not only is he long, but he's got girth!

Oh, he's going to fuck my brains out and I'm not going to be able to do anything but tremble in pleasure. "Calvin, I . . ." I say against his lips.

"What is it?" he asks, moving to kiss my shoulder and neck.

"I've never . . ." I close my eyes, hoping that'll give me the courage to say what I need. "I've never been with someone as big as you before."

He pulls his lips away and pushes himself up so he can look down at my face in the near-darkness. He offers up a sexy little smirk. "We'll just have to make sure you're good and ready then, won't we?" Without warning, he's down between my legs, pulling my panties off and tossing them over his shoulder. "Are you sure about this, Piper?" he asks from between my parted thighs.

I can't speak. All I can do is nod.

His lips find my inner knee and he slowly kisses his way up my thigh. Just when I think he's going straight to my core, he skips over it and moves to the other leg. He kisses down it just as slowly. Finally, he slowly runs his tongue along my slit. I can't help but jump when he brushes the tip of his tongue against my sensitive nub. My eyes flutter closed and I hear him let out a soft chuckle, but he doesn't stop. Instead, he dives in harder and faster, and just when I think I've caught on to his pattern, he changes it up—a tantalizing mix of flicks, sucks, and twirls.

I'm breathing heavily. He's going to think I'm having an asthma attack or something. But I can't think of that for long, because I may be having a heart attack with the way my heart is racing. Yep, pretty sure it just skipped a beat. My muscles tighten as that familiar tingle forms in my lower belly. As it spreads throughout me, my toes curl, my breathing stops, my heart freezes—or beats so fast I can't even feel it anymore. My release washes over me hot and heavy, and I can't help but call out his name over and over. I can't even manage to keep myself still. My back is arching off the bed like I'm being lifted up from my center. My legs are squeezing his head—holding him in place and quite possibility suffocating him. My hands are fisting the sheets, pulling and tugging on both sides of me. In the last year, I've been doing this myself, and my orgasm has lasted all of 20 seconds, but right now, it's been going for at least a minute. Just when I think I've hit the peak, it climbs higher and higher.

As the tingles start to fade away, everything gets easier to control. I lower my back and release Calvin's head from between my thighs. My fingers let go of the sheet and my whole body relaxes. Calvin pulls away and wipes at his glistening lips.

"Fuck, I thought I was going to suffocate down there," he says, breathless.

I can't hold in my giggle as I bring my hands to my face, attempting to cover it now that I can feel the heat radiating from it. "I'm sorry. I just . . . you're very good at that."

"That's not all I'm good at," he says, grabbing his pants off the floor. He pulls out his wallet and takes out a shiny foil wrapper. He stays between my legs—watching me as he rips it open and slides it over his length.

I watch in amazement as he rolls the condom down over himself. I half expect it to snap off like a rubber band that's stretched to its limit, but it doesn't. It rolls into place and I watch as he works his length up and down. "Still not backing out?" he asks as he lowers his body back to mine.

I reach for him, placing my hands on his sharp jaw as I direct him to my lips. "No way."

With his body fully on mine again, he's right where I need him.

He reaches between us and places himself at my opening. He gently pushes forward and already, I'm stretching around him.

I tense and squeeze his bicep.

"Just relax," he whispers, lowering his lips and pressing soft kisses down my neck as he slowly moves into me. I let out a soft whimper and he gently glides himself out before pushing in again. With each thrust, he goes just a little bit deeper, and my body quakes with the need to come again.

"Fuck, you're perfect, Piper," he breathes out against my skin.

I lace my fingers through his hair as he pumps into me, pushing me closer and closer to coming undone.

"Calvin, I'm almost there," I cry.

His hand moves between us, massaging my clit as he pushes deeper, harder, faster. My release builds and breaks free, shattering me into a million tiny pieces.

My headboard is banging off the wall and the box springs are squeaking beneath us. His skin is clapping off of mine and I'm moaning like a seasoned porn star. His heavy breathing and low grunts fill the room. Just as my release begins to fall away, every single one of his muscles tightens as his thrusts become more erratic. With one last jerk of his hips, he lets his release go until he's collapsing on top of me.

Neither one of us can move. My entire body is tingling and numb. My head feels like a balloon that's floating up above my body. Every hair is standing on end and vibrating. My heart is pounding so hard it just might jump right out of my chest, and his is the same way. I can feel it racing alongside my own.

He presses a kiss to my collarbone before withdrawing himself from me and lying at my side. He pulls off the condom and tosses it into the trash before lifting his right arm and sliding it beneath my head. I roll to my side, resting my head on his chest as I think over what we've just done.

I just had sex with my best friend's brother.

TEN

PIPER

I have so many questions rolling around in my head right now. Like, what the hell was that? Are we a thing now or was it just a hookup? Does Calvin have feelings for me? Deep down, have those feelings always been there? If they have, how must he have felt all these years when I was chasing his brother? Why would he keep picking me up time after time if he's always felt this way? Why hasn't he written me off already?

And Preston! What will he think of all of this? Will he be happy I've moved on? Will he be mad that it's with his own brother? Will he think that this is just me settling since I can't have him? It's all so confusing.

The one thing I am sure about, though, is what I'm feeling right now. There's excitement, fear, worry, bliss, but most of all, happiness and contentment. I thought after it was all said and done, there would be this awkwardness between us, but it's not awkward. It doesn't feel weird lying here in Calvin's arms. Instead, I feel safe and protected. He's soft and gentle. He doesn't find an excuse to run off like so many others I've been with.

He turns his head and presses a kiss to the top of my head. "What are you thinking?" he softly asks.

"I'm not."

"Nothing at all?"

"Nothing, but . . . that was amazing. Why didn't we do that sooner?" I joke.

He lets out a deep chuckle that rumbles throughout his chest. "I don't know, but we should have."

"Do you have to go?"

He looks over at the clock to see that it's pushing 3 a.m. "I can stay a while."

I smile to myself. "Good." I snuggle closer and close my eyes. I breathe his scent in deeply and it soothes everything away. Before I know it, I'm fast asleep, sleeping better than I ever have before.

I wake in the morning when my alarm goes off. I groan as I reach over to silence it. Once it's silent, I roll in the opposite direction, hoping I'll find Calvin beside me, but the bed is empty. In his place is a pink piece of paper from the notepad I keep by the bed. It reads:

PIPER,

Sorry I had to run off. It was getting late and I needed to get to work early. I'll lock the door behind me. And whatever you do, don't stress over what happened. Don't ruin the memory. Leave it as it is: perfect. Talk to you soon.

Calvin

I SMILE as I read over the note. Weirdly enough, it makes my body tingle all over again. I read it once more and giggle. He knows me so well. He knew that, left alone long enough, I would've overanalyzed everything that happened between us. I'm still wondering where this leaves us, but I won't jump to conclusions. I push the memory of last night out of my head as I stand and head toward the bathroom to shower and get ready for work.

An hour later, I'm walking out the door with my purse, laptop bag, and coffee. I put everything into the passenger seat and start the car. I'm backing out of the drive when my cell rings over the car speakers. I look at the screen and see his name. I smile as I accept the call.

"Hey."

"Good morning, beautiful. I was thinking I could bring over some takeout tonight and we could have our movie night. What do you think?"

I smile just from thinking about getting to spend another night in his arms. "Sounds great."

"Be there around 7 p.m.?"

"I'll see you then," I agree.

"Okay, I'll talk to you later."

"Calvin?"

"Yes?"

"I just wanted to say I had a lot of fun with you last night. And thank you for leaving that note. Sometimes it seems like you know me better than I do."

"I had a lot of fun with you too. Bye, beautiful."

He hangs up the phone and goosebumps prickle my skin just from hearing his voice and the way he called me beautiful. My gut reaction is to start picking this whole thing apart, but I refuse to let myself do that. I know that if I do, I'll freak out and panic, ruining whatever this is between us. And I'm nowhere near done.

Riley and I go out to lunch at our favorite sandwich shop. We're sitting at a table outside while we eat and drink our tea. "So, what did you do last night?" she asks, just to make conversation.

I don't answer but I feel my face grow 10 degrees hotter.

She smiles as she takes me in. "Tell me! I have to know now."

"Well, Calvin called yesterday while Preston was over. It was the first time Preston and I had talked since the whole ordeal. It wasn't long after Preston left that Calvin showed up to check on me and make sure I was okay. Then we may have . . . sort of . . . uh, we hooked up."

Her eyes grow wide as her mouth drops open. "You had sex with your best friend's brother? The best friend you just claimed to be in love with?"

I roll my eyes and nod. "Yes, but before you go ruining this, I need to say I didn't sleep with Cal as an attempt to get over Preston or as any kind of replacement. Got that?"

She holds up her hands, showing me her palms. "How do you explain it then?"

I take a bite out of my sandwich—chewing slowly and swallowing while thinking over my answer. "Okay, look, Calvin and I grew up together. I was closer to Preston than him, but still. Pres was the one I went to when I wanted to have fun and do something. But Calvin was the one I went to when I was hurt or in trouble. He's helped me out of every bad situation I've ever been in, which is why he showed up last night. He knew things between Preston and me weren't good. He wanted to make sure Preston didn't make them worse. And then, one thing just led to another. Lately—and I mean, before I even took Preston to that show—I've been having surprising feelings for Calvin."

"I don't think this was a random hookup, Piper."

"You don't?"

She shakes her head. "If everything you said is true, I think he's had feelings for you this whole time. I mean, what kind of guy is always there to pick up a girl who's down if he isn't in love with her?"

I roll my eyes. "That's just Calvin. He would do the same for you, or any woman, for that matter. He's sweet and kind. He's a gentleman."

"Show me a picture."

"What? No!"

"Come on. Show me or I'll just look him up on Insta."

I know she will, too. "Fine." I dig my phone out of my bag and search through the photos. His Insta account mostly advertises his law office. In every picture, he's in a tailored suit and looks professional. I want to show her a picture of him looking laid back and easygoing. I flip through the pictures on my phone until I find one of the three of us from my recent trip home. It's a picture I had our waitress snap after we'd finished eating.

In the picture, I'm between Preston and Calvin. I hand over the phone and watch as her eyes move from the screen, to me, and back. Her eyes widen and her lips turn up into a smile. "Girl, what's wrong with you? Calvin is wayyy hotter than Preston."

I giggle. "He kind of is, isn't he?" It's funny how I never really saw it before. And if I did see it, I was too blinded by Preston to fully accept it.

"This boy is in love with you."

I take my phone back and snort. "How do you know?" I look at the picture again.

"Look at the three of you. Preston has his arm over your shoulder like you're just any old buddy. But Calvin has his hand on your hip. And his fingers are curled slightly, like he's trying to pull you closer to him. He looks tall. Is he tall?"

I smile at the picture before putting my phone away and nod. "He is tall. He's tall and lean and . . . big." My eyes stretch wide and she giggles.

"How big?"

I lean in and whisper. "Bigger than anyone I've ever been with. Like, I-was-afraid-he'd-rip-me-in-two big."

She laughs and licks her lips like she's picturing it. "Lucky bitch," she breathes out jokingly.

The rest of the day passes unusually slowly. All I can think about is Calvin coming over tonight. I can't wait to cuddle up in his arms and spend the rest of the night beneath him. I'm a little sore today, but nothing that's going to stop me from enjoying him tonight.

I wonder if I should tell Preston that Calvin and I are spending so much time together, but at the same time, I don't want to tell him we're doing something we're not, and I don't exactly know what we're doing yet. This is all so new. I don't want to jinx anything. Plus, how would Preston react to the news that his older brother is screwing his best friend—the one who just confessed her love for him? I think it's best to keep this a secret for now.

When I finish up with work, I go home to take a shower and prepare for our movie night. I shave my legs, put on a touch of makeup, and blow-dry my hair. I put on a cute pair of pajama shorts —the kind that leaves the bottom of my booty hanging out slightly— and pair them with a tight white spaghetti strap top, sans bra. I'm reaching for a bottle of wine when the doorbell rings.

"It's open!" I call out as I grab a wine glass.

I hear it open and turn around expecting to see Calvin, but I'm surprised to see Preston instead. His eyes grow wide when he sees what I'm wearing.

I jump behind the island, trying to hide myself. "What are you doing here?" I ask in a panic.

He laughs. "You said to come in. What if I'd been the cable guy?"

"You were supposed to be who I'm waiting on right now."

"Oh, trying to get me out of your system by banging some other dude, huh?" He offers up a grin.

I force a smile. "Something like that. Now, if you don't need anything, I'm going to have to ask you to leave. I already have plans as you can see."

He laughs and nods. "Yeah, okay, just make sure he wraps it up well."

I shake my head as I walk out from behind the island and grab his bicep to lead him to the door. He thinks it's hilarious. "Damn, Pipes, you're looking good. Sure you don't want me to warm you up for him? I mean, I'll take one for the team if you know what I mean."

He's only joking, but it's annoying me, because I want him out before Calvin gets here. I don't know what it is we're doing yet, but I know I don't want anyone to know about it.

I open the door, ready to push Preston through it, but freeze when Calvin is on the other side. His icy eyes look me up and down with a smirk.

"Hey, man," Preston says, slapping him on the shoulder, "she's about to get laid, so you can't stay. She's already kicking me out."

I push him through the door.

Calvin smirks. "I won't stay long," he tells Preston. "But there is something we need to talk about," he adds on, looking at me.

I roll my eyes and open the door wider. "Better make it quick."

Preston laughs as he makes his way to his car. Calvin steps inside and the moment the door's shut, I find myself pressed against it. His mouth is on mine and my legs are wrapped around his waist. His hands are on my ass, caressing the soft skin my shorts don't cover.

"Is this how you normally dress for dinner and a movie?" he asks, assaulting my lips.

I offer up a flirty smile. "I figured I'd want to be comfy for a night on the couch. You like?"

"I love," he agrees, moving his mouth back to mine. His lips move from mine down to my neck and upper chest. Finally, he takes a deep breath and pulls away. "The food should be here any minute and I'd rather not answer the door with an erection."

I giggle. "Good thinking. The poor delivery boy would probably think you're hiding a weapon in there to rob him."

He rolls his eyes as he sets me on my feet. "Very funny."

Even though I'm standing, I don't release my arms from around his neck. "I guess I could answer the door . . . that way, we could keep doing this," I say, letting one hand glide down his chest toward his pants, where he catches my hand.

"If you think I'm letting another man see you like this, you're crazy. It's bad enough my brother got a look at you." He reaches up and traces the outline of my nipple through my shirt. It hardens immediately.

I snort. "Preston saw the whole package long ago."

"My brother's seen you naked? Remind me to punch him for that later," he says around a smile.

I open my mouth to say something, but someone knocks on the door.

"Go get the wine, and I'll grab the food," Calvin says, watching me walk away.

I find two glasses and a bottle of wine. When I walk back into the living room, he's already arranging the food on the table. I set down the bottle and two glasses.

"Where's the movie? I'll put it in."

He opens his jacket and pulls the movie out of the inner pocket, handing it over. I move to the TV and put in the DVD. When I turn around, he's taking off his jacket and tie.

I walk up to him and look in his eyes as I start to unbutton his shirt.

He smirks. "What are you doing?"

"It's movie night. We can't stuff our faces with Chinese food if you're wearing a suit and dress shirt. Let me help you with that." I unbutton his shirt and push it over his shoulders, revealing the undershirt beneath. I grab his belt and unfasten it, pulling it off in one swift motion. I look at his pants. They don't look comfortable, but what can we do about that now? "You need to bring some more comfortable clothes over here for occasions like this."

He rolls his eyes. "I was hoping to end up naked anyway."

"Oh, we'll get there. But I don't think eating hot sauce while naked is a good idea."

The two of us take our seats on the couch and start the movie. I'm surprised to find that Calvin has managed to procure all of my favorite selections. There's orange chicken, fried rice, eggs rolls, lo mein noodles, and extra packets of soy sauce. I pick up an egg roll and add some soy sauce. "How did you know what to get? This is always my exact order."

He smirks as he eats his grilled chicken and white rice. "I figured anything fried was a must."

I laugh and shake my head, playfully smacking him across the chest.

"You're a medical mystery. How anyone can consume alcohol and eat nothing but fried foods as much as you and still have *that* figure is beyond me."

I give him a bigger smile than necessary. "I'm one of a kind."

After we eat, the food gets pushed away as we lie on the couch watching the movie. I'm wedged between the back of the couch and Calvin's chest, resting my head on his toned pec. His hand is absent-mindedly running through my hair.

"You know what's funny?" I ask him.

"What's that?"

"That weekend we all spent at home, my dad said something about how I needed to find a man like you, and Preston burst out laughing. He said we're complete opposites and that we'd never get along long enough to have a relationship."

"And what did you say?"

I smile as I remember. "I said we'd have to connect on a deeper level. That, or you'd have to be really good in bed." I giggle out the last part.

"And which one stands true?"

"Both," I answer, turning my head to look up at him.

His hand moves up to cup my cheek, holding me in place as his lips move to mine. They're soft and strong and warm and sweet. He kisses me slowly, teasingly. He's not pushing for more. He's simply enjoying having his lips on mine. But the longer we kiss, the more my body tingles and comes to life. I find myself crawling up his body, moving to straddle him.

His hands find my hips and he squeezes them tightly, gently grinding me against his hardness.

"Take me to bed, Calvin," I whisper into our kiss.

On demand, he holds me tightly against him as he stands and walks us into my room. He lays me down and covers my body with his, kissing his way up to my lips while our hands messily rip off each other's clothing.

When we're fully undressed, he kisses his way down my body,

just like he did last night, but I stop him before he gets to my center. I place my hand on his jaw and tilt his head up until his icy blue eyes are locked on mine.

"I want to taste you tonight, Calvin."

"Are you sure?" he asks, sounding a little nervous.

I'm quite aware of the mouthful he has going on, but I'm absolutely sure. I nod.

He climbs back up my body, pressing kisses along the way until he's at my side. I sit up and get between his legs, watching his face as I unbutton and unzip his pants. He lifts his hips and allows me to pull them down to his thighs. His hard cock springs free and stands at attention. I work my hand up and down the silky skin as I wet my lips. I look at him one last time as I'm going down. His eyes are hooded with desire, burning with passion.

I slide his tip into my mouth and run my tongue around it. He takes a hissing breath. Slowly, I work my way down his length, using my hand to pump what can't fit down my throat. I've never been turned on by a man's moans, but Calvin's are like nothing I've ever heard. They're a mix of heavy breathing, whispered pleas, and soft whimpers. He has one hand fisted in my hair, while the other is tangled in the sheet. It doesn't take long before he's pleading with me to stop, but I don't. I want to taste his release. I want his sweetness on my tongue. I want to taste what I do to him.

With one last warning, his orgasm washes over him and he spills himself into my mouth. I swallow down every squirt he gives me while continuing to suck. When it's clear there's nothing left, I pull back, ready to slide a condom down his length, but his hand that's tangled in my hair pulls me upward, his mouth landing on mine.

I know a lot of men won't kiss a girl after she's gone down on them, but Calvin isn't afraid or holding back. He kisses me hard—so full of passion. While I'm seeing stars from our kiss, his cock grows stiff again, and it presses against my opening like it has a mind of its own. I move my hips against him, trailing his tip between my folds and spreading my wetness. When his hand reaches up and pinches my hard nipple, I'm no longer in control. I push down on him, sliding him inside me. We both let out relieved moans at the connection.

Instead of telling me to stop or get a condom, his hands land on my hips, lifting me up and dropping me back down his length until I can take all of him. I never knew how good it felt to be stretched so tightly. There's pain, but there's so much pleasure, and it mixes together like a delicious cocktail. I grind my clit against his pubic bone, and before I know it, I'm shattering on top of him, coming undone in every way possible.

When my release ends, he lifts me up and flips me over, entering me from behind. This position makes him feel even bigger, and it has me moaning and panting as he pushes me over the edge again.

He still doesn't let himself go. He pulls out of me and lays me on my back, positioning himself between my thighs. He slides into me as his chest presses against mine. He kisses me softly and slowly, and I can't help but notice the difference. Before was rough and hard and rushed. Now he's taking his time with me and savoring the experience. Both ways feel amazing, and I can't help but hold on to him, kiss him back, and cry out his name.

ELEVEN

CALVIN

I'm absolutely fucking lost in her. I've never craved a woman as badly as I want her. I've never gone back for seconds—not unless we were actually dating and in some sort of relationship. But Piper and I haven't discussed what this is—what *we* are. I don't want to push her to jump into something she isn't ready for. I mean, less than a week ago, she thought she was in love with my little brother. And now, here we are, fucking without a condom.

I don't know if I'm sort of a Band-Aid to cover the pain Preston left behind, but right now, I couldn't care less. I'll be whatever she needs me to be, as long as I get to have her for a little while. Sure, I hope this opens her eyes and she realizes what she thought she felt for Preston was nothing more than some silly crush. I hope she realizes I've been there for her throughout the years because I'm in love with her. I hope this is the start of a long relationship for us, and that we can move on to getting married, having kids, and growing old together. But I don't have my hopes up. Right now, all I can think about is keeping myself buried in her for as long as possible.

I pump into her until I can't hold back another second. Then it dawns on me that I'm not wearing a condom and we didn't talk about how this would end. Should I pull out? Since the rules haven't been discussed, it's better to be safe than sorry. When my release makes its way to the surface, I pull out and use my hand to pump myself up and down, spilling every last drop onto her stomach. My heart is racing and my lungs are doubling their efforts to get me the oxygen I need. I rest my head on the pillow between her head and shoulder while keeping my body off of hers until I can get up to grab a towel.

She runs her hand through my hair, gently tugging at the strands. I lift my head and kiss her softly. "I'll go get a towel." I give her one last quick kiss before removing myself from her completely and walking into the connected bathroom. I use the bathroom and wash my hands before studying my reflection in the mirror. My eyes are lit up with happiness and the usual soft lines around my eyes have faded away. With her, there's no effort. I don't have to try or force anything. I feel like when we're together, we're still just a couple of kids.

I turn away from my reflection and grab a towel, taking it back to the bed. I sit on the edge and wipe her stomach clean, then toss the towel onto the floor and lie at her side. Without having to ask, she rolls into me, wrapping me up in her arms and legs and holding me close. I can feel her heart pounding against my side even though her breathing has evened out. Her warmth sinks into me and I know this is exactly where I want to spend the rest of my life.

I run my hand up and down her back as we both try to calm our bodies. There's nothing but silence, but it's a comfortable one. There's no awkwardness between us. Only comfort, acceptance, and maybe even love.

"Can I ask you a question?" she asks, breaking the silence.

I chuckle. "I think you already did."

I practically hear her eyes roll. "Have you always felt this way about me?"

Ah, the dreaded question. Because now I have to explain that while she was chasing after my brother, I had to sit back and watch. Every time, it broke my heart a little more. "Well, I wouldn't say *always*. It's been going on for years though."

"I'm so sorry I never saw it. You must have felt awful every time I came to you crying about how Preston didn't have feelings for me."

"It wasn't awful, because each time you did, it gave me hope that it would be the last time—that you'd finally wake up and move on from him."

She doesn't reply, so I ask, "This thing we're doing, have you ever thought about it before?"

She takes a deep breath and lets it out slowly. "Growing up, I didn't see you like that. You were older and weren't around much by the time I really started looking at boys. I remember there being a few times when you came home from college and I stood back and thought, 'Wow, he's really growing up.' But that was it. Until your recent phone call."

"What phone call?" I ask, confused.

"When Preston and I were leaving the beach and you called because you were on your way home too. You laughed about something—I don't remember what—but it made my body come alive. There were tingles and I was so confused because: one, I couldn't even see you, and two, you were Calvin. I couldn't have feelings for Calvin. That night, I was so nervous to go out with you guys. And even though I tried to focus on Preston, you kept stealing my attention. I couldn't deny how good-looking you were and the effect you seemed to have on me."

"So this isn't just because Preston is no longer an option for you?" I ask and feel stupid for doing so. This one question could ruin whatever it is we're doing.

She rolls onto her stomach and looks up at me. Her green eyes are shining and the corners of her pink lips are turned slightly upward. "This—you and me—has nothing to do with Preston. If anything, he just took himself out of the picture so I could see you more clearly. You no longer have that filter over you. Everything is stripped away now. I can see you for you. And when I look at you, I see the guy who was always there to pick me up when I needed him most. Even when I didn't know I needed him."

I don't know what I was expecting, but her answer is perfect and I press my lips to hers again—a kiss that's long and deep. When it ends, she lays her head back on my chest and I run my fingers through her honey-colored curls.

"I want to take you out. On a real date."

I feel her cheek move against my chest when she smiles. "I'd like that," she agrees.

In the morning, I have to leave early again in order to make it to work on time. I'm used to living in the heart of the city, and being able to roll of out bed, shower, dress, and drive a few blocks to get to the office. But her place isn't in the center of the city like my apartment. It's off in the suburbs. If I don't get a head start, I'll be stuck in traffic all morning. I quickly write her a note and get on my way as I plan our date night.

———

I MANAGE to have a dress delivered to her office with shoes, jewelry, and flowers. The attached card explains that tonight is date night and I have everything covered. It's going on noon when she calls.

"Calvin, this is too much. You don't have to do all of this, you know."

"I know I don't, but I wanted to. Everything is planned out. All you have to do is show up."

"You're so stupid," she says, but I hear her smile and know that's her little way of saying I love you without using those words.

"I'll see you at 7 p.m." I hang up the phone and see that I have a text confirming our reservation at the Capital Grille. I also got us the best room at the Gwen, and it's already being prepared for our arrival. I've ordered chocolate-covered strawberries, champagne, rose petals, and a nice hot, bubble bath in the deep porcelain tub. Tonight is going to be the most romantic night of Piper's life. I'm going to make sure of it.

After getting all the preparations ready, I start to think about all the guys she's dated. Her first boyfriend's name was Bryan. He was on the baseball team and was friends with Preston. I think he set them up, but he also broke them up when Preston felt Pipes was too busy to hang out with him anymore. At the time, I thought it was funny. I thought that maybe watching her with another guy had made him realize he wanted her too, but that wasn't the case.

Then she dated Matt, the quarterback. He was the one who escorted her to her junior prom and took her virginity. When Preston found out, he beat the shit out of him and was suspended from the team for a week. I thought that was funny too. I assumed it would open his eyes for certain, but sure enough, he was just as blind as ever.

I don't know much about the guys she dated in college, because she and Preston weren't together much. I know he mentioned her dating some yacht-owning asshole, but as far as I know, they didn't last long.

I guess my only real competition romance-wise would've been from Richie Rich, since I know a couple of high school kids never could've pulled off something like this. I want to impress her. I want her to see that there's nothing I wouldn't do for her. No distance I wouldn't walk for her. I just want her to see that I'm absolutely sure about us and where we're going, even if it is still new.

When I get home from work, I strip out of my suit and go for a shower. I wash and shave my face, style my hair, and wrap a towel around my waist as I head into my walk-in closet to find something to wear. I'm surprised when, as I'm walking past my open bedroom door, I find Preston sitting on the couch in the living room. I pause, take a step back, and do a double take to ensure I'm not seeing things.

"What are you doing here?" I ask, finally walking into the living room.

"I let myself in. The door was unlocked."

I study him, wondering what the hell he's doing.

"You got plans tonight? I snagged tickets to see The Killers at the last minute, but Piper refuses to go with me. Something about seeing that guy from the other night. Speaking of which, did you get a peek at him while you were there?"

I shake my head. "No, she made me leave before he arrived."

"Damn, I wonder who she's seeing. And why is she keeping him hidden? I mean, it's not like I'm going to chase the guy off."

I sit on the couch. "If I remember correctly, you've chased off all her boyfriends."

"I know, and looking back, that probably wasn't a good idea. But they weren't good enough for her. If she's hiding this guy, she must be ashamed or something. He's probably just another loser."

"Or maybe she wants to get to know him a little better before introducing you two. You know, to ensure you won't chase this one away too."

He snorts. "I'll only chase him off if he isn't good enough. I don't want her getting stuck with some unemployed loser who will just use her for her money and sleep with all her girlfriends."

I shrug, not sure what to say. I need to appear to be on his side so I don't raise suspicion, but I'm on Piper's side on this one.

"So, anyway, about tonight?" he asks, raising his brow, blue eyes hopeful.

"Sorry, man. I can't. I have a business dinner at the Capital Grille."

"Blow it off!"

"I can't, Pres. This is a new client. I can't reschedule our first meeting. I'd lose the chance for sure. I'm sorry, but I'm sure you'll find someone." I walk him toward the door, not giving him a chance to argue. At the last second, I push him through it and close it in his face, locking it this time so he can't walk in again.

I dress in my nicest suit and get a call when the limo has arrived. I go downstairs and climb into the back seat, setting the bouquet of flowers on the seat next to me. For the next hour, I sit and wait as the driver navigates through evening traffic. Finally, the limo arrives at her house, and I grab the flowers to take to the door.

She opens it wearing the dress I picked out. She looks gorgeous.

The white dress ends at her knee, the skirt loose and flowing around her tanned legs. The top of the dress has amazing beadwork that sparkles and shimmers when the light hits it. It's low-cut, but still respectable, and sleeveless, showing off those sun-kissed shoulders of hers. Her hair is beautiful—half pulled back so it doesn't hide her face, but still long and curled as it hangs down her back. She's put on makeup, but it isn't a lot. It's just enough to highlight her features and showcase my favorite part: her sparkling green eyes.

"You look . . . beautiful," I breathe out.

She smiles. "Are those for me?" She nods toward the forgotten flowers I'm holding at my side.

"Oh, yeah." I hold them out and she takes them with a giggle. She brings them to her nose and inhales their scent before grabbing a vase and filling it with water before adding the flowers. Then she smiles as she loops her arm through mine and we walk to the awaiting limo. I allow her to crawl in first, then I slide in behind her. The door closes and we're alone.

"Wine?" I ask, grabbing the bottle.

"Sure." She smiles and it steals my breath while making my heart beat harder. "You really didn't have to do all of this, Calvin. It's too much."

"It's not too much." I hand her a glass. "It's perfect. Tonight is all about you relaxing." I clink my glass off of hers and we each take a sip.

She giggles and says, "We need to figure out what we're going to do about Preston. He's driving me crazy. I basically had to kick him out of my house when I told him I couldn't go to the concert with him. Then he demanded to know the name of the person I'm dating."

I laugh. "I know. He came by my place too."

"What did you tell him?"

"That I had a business dinner with a new client." I take another drink. "What do you want to tell him?"

"Honestly, right now, I don't want to tell him anything. I like being in our own little bubble, don't you?"

"I just like being with you, Piper."

She gives me a small smile. "I just want to be sure of what we're doing before we tell everyone. You know what everyone is going to think—that I'm just with you because I couldn't get Preston. Things are still so early and everything's going great. I don't want anyone coming between us."

"So you want to wait?"

She nods her head. "If that's okay with you."

I pick up her hand and press a kiss to the back. "I'll do anything you want, as long as I get to spend time with you like this. Just us. No Preston. No expectations. No strings. Just us."

"I'll drink to that," she says, knocking her glass off mine and taking a drink.

The drive to the restaurant seems to go by in no time now that I have her beside me. We touch and kiss and laugh on our way to dinner. The ride ends far too soon for my liking, but I get the whole night with her.

We go into the restaurant and are seated right away. She looks around the place in amazement. "I've never been here before."

"No?" I ask as I'm pushing in her chair.

She shakes her head. "No, I'm usually found around coffee carts and taco bars."

I laugh as I take my seat across from her. "Well, this place is amazing. Order anything and everything you want."

The waiter comes over and I order us a bottle of wine while she reads over the menu. We end up settling on crab cakes to start, then she orders some kind of pasta for dinner. Dessert is the best. We share a triple chocolate brownie topped with chocolate syrup, whipped cream, and nuts. By the time I'm paying the bill and we're leaving, I couldn't eat another bite.

As the two of us are walking out, we bump into Preston. He looks me up and down, then does the same to Piper. "What the hell are you two doing here? I thought you said you had a date?" he asks her.

"Uh, I lied," she says, not sounding very convincing.

He looks at me. "And I thought you said you had a business dinner."

"I did," I lie. "My new client is Piper." I just blurted it out without thinking it through. Fuck.

His face wrinkles. "Piper?" He looks at her. "Why do you need a lawyer?"

Her eyes are wide with fear and panic. "Um, I need a lawyer because . . . I'm suing you!" she announces.

He looks taken aback. "Suing me?" he points at his chest.

She looks like she's kicking herself.

"Why would you sue me?"

"Because you humiliated me on that show! I'm suing for de . . . what's it called?" She looks at me.

"Defamation?" I ask, trying to play along with her story.

"Defam . . . *what?*" he asks, looking between the two of us. "What the hell does that mean?"

"Oh, and emotional distress. That too," she adds on. I can tell she's proud of herself for coming up with this plan on the spot—anything to protect our secret.

"You have emotional distress? From me? If you sue, I'm countersuing."

I hold up my hands. "Okay, now wait a minute. We discussed it over dinner and I've managed to talk Piper out of the lawsuit. Right, Piper?"

She looks at me, surprised I'm taking his side, but then she quickly realizes she doesn't actually want to sue Preston. She nods. "That's right. You'd better suck up to your brother, cause your ass would've been getting handed to you right now."

I can't help the smirk that pulls at my lips.

"Piper, you were really going to sue me?" He sounds a little hurt.

She rolls her eyes. "Don't take it so personally, Preston. I was just trying to teach you a lesson. I doubt it would've gone to trial."

He scoffs, mouth hanging open. "Whatever. So are you two free now? We can grab some drinks and hang out, and you can tell me more about why you wanted to take me to court."

"I actually have to get back home. I have an early morning."

I nod. "Yeah, me too. We can catch up in a day or two."

The two of us walk out, keeping as much distance between us as possible before making our way to the limo once Preston is out of sight.

We drive around the city for a little while, sipping our wine, and watching the lights on the fountain change colors before finally heading to the hotel.

"I didn't know I needed to pack for an overnight trip."

I shoot her a grin. "That's okay. You won't need clothes for what I have planned." I step out and offer her my hand.

TWELVE

PIPER

The whole night has been absolutely perfect. Dinner was amazing and I stuffed myself completely full. Running into Preston wasn't great, but I think I covered for us well. I could have died laughing from the face he made when I said I was going to sue him. It's a good thing I can think on my toes. I even surprised Calvin.

He takes me up to our suite and it's gorgeous. There's a fancy sitting room that looks like a living room. There's a full kitchen and dining area, and a bedroom with a balcony that overlooks the city.

There's a trail of rose petals leading the way to the bed, and I follow them until I'm in the bedroom, where I reach behind me to unzip my dress. Calvin walks up to my back and presses a kiss to my neck as his hand lowers the zipper.

"We have a nice, hot bath waiting for us," he says softly in my ear.

I can't help the embarrassment that stains my cheeks as my dress falls down my body to the floor. I made sure to wear the sexiest bra and panty set I had. They're both white, made of lace, and completely see-through. I go to take a step toward the bathroom, but he stops me with a hand on my hip.

"I know there's a bath waiting, but all I can think about is ripping this thong off with my teeth." He presses his lips to my neck as his hand quickly unsnaps my bra, which joins my dress in the pile on the floor.

I spin around to face him—I'm nearly naked while he's still completely dressed. I reach up, grabbing his tie. "It's looks like you're a little overdressed for the occasion, Mr. Young." I loosen the tie and push his jacket over his shoulders.

He lets out a growl as he shrugs out of the jacket and tears off the tie. In the next second, he's pulling me against him and kissing me senseless.

The rest of the night is spent in a mix of bubbles, champagne, giggles, touches, and kisses. Oh, and plenty of lovemaking time and time again.

———

I WAKE IN THE MORNING, and to my surprise, Calvin is still next to me. I smile as I cuddle close to his side, happy he didn't run off to work like he usually does. "Good morning, sleepyhead," I say, pressing kisses to his jaw and neck.

He lets out a soft moan as he stretches. "A guy could get used to this."

The butterflies in my stomach take flight as I kiss lower—down his naked chest to the spot that's so happy to see me. I'm only beneath the sheet for a moment before he's pulling me back up his body and sliding into me from underneath.

Checkout is at noon, and we somehow manage to pull away from each other. The limo is already parked and waiting out front. I feel like I'm doing the walk of shame as I stroll through the nice hotel in my evening dress, but Calvin doesn't seem to notice the looks we're getting. We climb back into the limo and he takes my hand in his.

"This was perfect, Calvin. I'm a little sad to see it end."

He kisses my head as he pulls me closer. "Stick with me, beautiful, and it'll never have to." He kisses me softly. The only thing I can think about is how lucky I am to have him—to have always had him even when I didn't realize it.

Since it's Saturday and there's no work to be done, I spend the day cleaning up my house and catching up on laundry. Calvin promised to join me after going home to shower and change.

He calls a little while later to cancel, saying he has something at work that needs attention and that he'll be over by dinnertime. I'm a little sad that I won't get the whole day with him. I'm sitting on the couch and mindlessly flipping through the TV channels when an idea hits me.

If Calvin can't come to me, then maybe I should go to him. I could show up in a sexy outfit and seduce him from under his desk. The thought sounds too good to be true. I jump up quickly and rush to my room to get ready.

I curl my hair to perfection and paint my face more than I normally would. I line my green eyes darkly, doing the smoky-eye look with my shadow and adding false lashes. I apply a thick layer of bright red lipstick and slip on my darkest sunglasses before standing back and looking myself over. I'm wearing a long trench coat. The only thing beneath it is a black lace thong, a garter, and stockings. I put on the highest pair of pumps I have and hit the road.

When I walk into the building, there's no one behind the front desk, so I head straight to his office. I take off my coat and sling it over the couch. I decide to sit in his desk chair and prop my feet up on his desk. One of his ties is hanging on the coat rack, so I grab it and put it on. It sits right between my breasts and I know he'll love it.

It's while I'm sitting at his desk, looking around at all his hard work, that I realize the brother I'm truly in love with is Calvin. He's always been the one, even when I was too dumb to see it. He's been there through it all. He's sexy, amazing, smart, talented, and he loves me. I know he does. If he didn't, we wouldn't be where we are right now. He would've written me off long ago and found someone else to be with. The fact that he's still single isn't a fluke. He's been waiting for me. And I fully intend on telling him the moment he walks through that door.

I hear the sounds of a man's voice as he walks closer to the door. My body goes on high alert. This is it: the moment we've all been waiting for. The door opens and I suck in a breath, making my chest rise and look even fuller. Calvin walks in and his eyes land on mine. His double in size as he takes in the picture before him. Then the worst happens. Another man walks in behind him. He looks from Calvin, to me, and back. Then back again because *hello!* I'm practically naked here.

I jump up quickly and rush for my coat, pulling it against my chest as I try hiding from the man.

"Piper, what are you doing here?" Calvin asks, rushing to help cover me up.

I look at him and can feel the tears of embarrassment filling my eyes. "I'm sorry. I thought you'd be alone. I shouldn't have come." Without another word, I pull away from him and head toward the door as quickly as possible. However, my long coat gets tangled around my heel and I trip and fall, nearly taking the other man down as I try walking past him. He catches me and helps me get back on my feet.

"Thank you. I'm sorry." I turn back to Calvin as my feet carry me away. "I'm so sorry."

I'm nearly to my car when the tears finally overfill my eyes. I quickly wipe them away, not caring if I smear my makeup as I peel out of the parking lot as fast as my car will let me.

Back home, I strip everything off and climb into the bathtub with a bottle of wine. I haven't attempted to fix my makeup, so I have big black streaks going down my cheeks. I'm nearly drunk when the bathroom door opens. I jump but relax as soon as my eyes land on Calvin.

I see him and the tears fall all over again. "I'm so sorry, Calvin. I didn't mean to embarrass you. I just thought it would be a fun surprise. I never imagined you'd have someone with you. Was he a client? Did I cost you a job?"

He sits on the closed toilet and laughs. "No, he's an old friend from college. We were discussing a partnership. And you didn't scare him off. I think he only agreed to my terms because of you."

"Really?" I ask, feeling hopeful. "He was embarrassed for you?"

"Embarrassed? No way. I think he was jealous you were there for me and not him." He smiles and his icy eyes light up.

I breathe a heavy sigh of relief.

"I am wondering, though, what made you decide to do that." He grabs a washcloth and moves to sit on the floor beside the tub. He dips it, wrings it out, then starts to wipe at the smeared makeup streaking my face.

I shrug, suddenly feeling shy and embarrassed. This isn't how I wanted to tell him—with him coming to my rescue yet again. So instead of telling him how I really feel, I simply say, "I just wanted to spend the day with you. I wanted to surprise you."

He offers up a sweet smile as he wipes under my eyes. "I'm all yours for the rest of the day. I do wish you were still in that little costume though. I have to admit, that tie looked better on you."

I laugh. I knew he'd love seeing that. "Well, I don't have that getup on anymore, but I do have something better."

"What's that?"

"How about a completely naked bubble bath?" I wag my brows at him and he chuckles, stands up, then begins to strip out of his suit to join me in the tub.

After our bath and a good romp in the sheets, we both pull on our clothes and go to the kitchen in search of a late lunch. We snack on fruit, veggies, and cheese, paired with a bottle of wine—enough to hold us over until we order dinner. I get busy cutting the cheese into cubes while Calvin cuts carrots into sticks. I've already opened a bottle of wine and poured a little into two glasses. We lay out a platter with crackers and grapes, and I can't wait to dig in.

"We should make Bloody Marys," I suggest as I pop a cheese cube into my mouth.

"That sounds good. We can add that to breakfast in the morning."

"Alcohol with breakfast?" I act appalled that he would even suggest such a thing.

"Not you, Mr. Strait-Laced," I joke.

He laughs. "Wait until you see me on vacation. It's nothing but mixed drinks and a constant buzz the whole time."

"That's something I want to see," I say, placing a grape between my lips and leaning forward so he can take it. He does and gives me a kiss.

"I think summer would be a great time to take a trip to Hawaii. What do you think? A whole week of nothing but lying on the beach, getting drunk, and having sex while working on your tan?"

I smile just from thinking about the amazing time we'd have. "That sounds perfect. But sex only in the room. I don't need any weird tan lines," I joke.

The front door opens and Preston walks into the kitchen. "Having a party and didn't invite me?" He acts offended as he grabs a glass of wine and takes a big swig. He puts the empty glass down and scoffs. "That shit is nasty. Where's the beer, Pipes?" He moves around us and opens the fridge.

"Help yourself," I mumble, feeling a little annoyed that he's here to crash our party. Since I don't want to break the news to him until we for sure have something to break, we're still keeping our relationship a secret. Which means no touching or kissing.

Preston grabs a beer, pops the top, and takes a long drink. He studies Calvin and me. "Since when did you join the likes of him and his sensitive palate?" he asks, motioning toward the food and wine.

I frown at him. "There's nothing wrong with laying off the cheap beer and enjoying a nice glass of wine every once in a while, Pres."

Preston shoots Calvin a glare. "You're ruining my best friend."

Calvin chuckles and shakes his head as he places some carrots on the tray. "Maybe she's not your best friend anymore. Maybe she's mine. Have you thought of that, Pres?"

My eyes cut over to Calvin, who seems to be challenging Preston. Preston looks taken aback but not angry. "I guess we'll just have to share her then," he says, wrapping his arm around my shoulders and pulling me into a headlock.

I don't miss my shot to smack him in the junk with the back of my hand. He immediately releases me while he groans and cups his manhood.

Calvin laughs at the cheap shot. "All right, you two. Let's sit on the patio and enjoy this spread." He picks up the tray and walks toward the patio. I fill my glass of wine and pick up Calvin's to take outside. Preston follows along, holding his junk and keeping his beer close.

The three of us sit at the patio table and I grab a carrot to snack on.

"So, what you been up to, Pres?" Calvin asks, taking a sip of his wine.

He shrugs. "Not much. What about you?"

Calvin sets his glass down and grabs a grape, quickly glancing at me before answering. "Well, I've made a deal with an old friend from college. We're going to be partners and share the office."

Preston frowns. "That's your office. Why would you want to share it?"

Calvin looks me in the eye as he answers. "So I'll have more free time." I get what he's saying, and it makes the butterflies in my stomach take flight. "I'm staying busy. Too busy." He tears his gaze from me and looks at his brother. "I want someone to pick up the slack and maybe even take a little off my plate so I can have more time to do the things I enjoy. Spend more time with the people I love. In fact, with his buy-in, I'll be able to afford a nice vacation this year. I'm thinking Hawaii." He looks at me again, this time with a grin.

"Well, good for you," Preston says. "Hawaii sounds awesome." He nudges me. "Hey, maybe we should go with. Leave Calvin here to be an old man lounging on the beach. Then we could go off on our own adventures."

I smile and nod. "Sounds good, but I don't know if I'll be able to take time off work for something like that." I look up at Calvin. "When are you going?"

He shrugs as he leans back in his chair. "I don't have anything set in stone. We have to finalize this deal first and get everything situated. I'm thinking August, though, if everything goes smoothly."

"That would give you plenty of advance notice to put in for time off," Preston says, nudging me.

I laugh. "Did you ever think that maybe Calvin doesn't want us to go on his trip? That maybe there's someone special he wants to take instead? Plus, I don't know if I'll be able to afford it—the cost of the airfare, a hotel, the amount I'd spend on eating and drinking alone . . . not to mention, I wouldn't be getting paid that week since I've used up my vacation time already."

Preston takes a beat then asks, "I've never known you to turn down an adventure. What's happened to you lately?"

He's clearly confused and has every right to be. If I didn't have to hide this secret from him, I never would've second-guessed it. I would've accepted in a heartbeat.

"We all have to grow up at some point, Pres." I take a sip of my wine, feeling a little mad at myself for letting him down, but I guess that's something I'm going to have to get used to. I've always agreed to everything he's suggested, hoping it would finally lead to us getting together. But that's no longer the case. Now it's Calvin I don't want to let down. Will I always feel like I have to choose between them? Pick my best friend or the guy I'm falling madly in love with? If we move forward, will I have to choose between my friend and my husband?

"Well, whatever," Preston says, standing. "I'll catch up with you guys later." He walks back into the house to leave out the front door.

I let out a long sigh when I hear the front door close and his car start up a few minutes later.

"What's the matter?" Calvin asks.

I shrug and eat a grape. "I don't know. Keeping us a secret is harder than I thought it would be."

He sits up and reaches across the table for my hand. "We don't have to hide if you don't want to. All we have to do is tell him. I'm sure he'll be happy for us."

"I know . . . I just don't want to tell him anything until we're sure about us."

"I'm sure. Aren't you sure?"

"Well, I thought I was . . ."

His brows lift. "You *thought* you were?"

"It's just that this conversation with Preston brought something to my attention."

"And what's that?"

"Will I always be stuck between my best friend and the guy I'm seeing? If we move on to get married, will I have to choose between my best friend and my husband—not only ruining our relationship with each other, but with your whole family as well since my best friend and the guy I'm with are brothers?"

I feel a sudden panic creeping up my throat and Calvin sits back and takes a deep breath, trying to wrap his head around my concerns and how to fix them like he always has. "Are you saying, hypothetically, that if you had to choose between your best friend and me, you'd choose your best friend?"

"No, I'm not saying that. It would depend on the situation. I mean, if Preston wanted to go to a baseball game and you wanted to go dancing, I'd choose whichever activity I wanted to do. Sometimes I might side with you and sometimes I might side with him."

"So what are you worried about?" He stands up and scoots his chair closer to mine. He rests his elbows on his knees as he leans forward, holding my hands between his.

"I don't know. I just don't want to be put in a position where I have to choose between the two of you. I mean, if you were to say right now, 'It's me or him,' I don't know what I'd do, because he's been my best friend for my whole life and you—while we've only just started doing this thing we're doing—you already mean so much to me."

He shakes his head, cutting off my rambling. "I would never do that, Piper." He pulls me closer, pressing his lips to mine.

While he said *he'd* never do that, it doesn't mean Preston never would. I don't get time to think of all the ways this could backfire, because his tongue is now in my mouth and I can't think of anything else.

THIRTEEN

CALVIN

I t's been one month of spending every night with Piper. I feel like I've finally gotten everything I've ever wanted. We've been insep-arable. If I'm not staying at her place, she's staying at mine, only parting to go to our jobs. But when we meet back up at the end of every day, it's like no time has passed. Every night, I hold her close. Every morning, I wake up to her smiling face. If anything, I'm only falling more in love with her. Before, I craved her. Now, I'm addicted to her.

We're still keeping our little secret from Preston and our families. We've talked about it many times. Our parents are the best of friends and do everything together. Not to mention, my brother is her best friend and has been since childhood. There's a lot on the line for us. Even if something happens and we don't work out, we don't want our families punished for it. We intend to keep our relationship on the down low until we're absolutely sure we're spending the rest of our lives together.

You'd think with so much time spent together that keeping this secret from Preston would be hard, but it hasn't been as bad as I thought it'd be. He's been really caught up in work lately, plus he has a few different girls on the side to keep him busy. The two of us have only spoken to him over the phone, and it's always been a quick conversation, mostly just checking in more than anything.

But this afternoon, we're leaving to spend the weekend at home for the annual Fourth of July party. Piper's parents always go all out for the holiday. There's a big swimming party in their in-ground pool. We cook, drink, laugh, and have fun until dark when we light up the neighborhood with fireworks. We know we're going to have to keep our distance somewhat, and neither of us is looking forward to it, but it's what we have to do until the time is right.

The two of us take off work early Thursday afternoon to make the drive. We'll both be staying at our parents' homes like usual, but after spending so many nights together, we aren't looking forward to sleeping alone. Tomorrow, she's volunteered to help her mom with all the food prep and party decorations for Saturday. Whatever time we do get will have to be stolen.

It's going on 2 p.m. when we're both back at her place with our bags packed. She has her suitcase sitting by the door when I walk in.

"Hey!" I call out, not finding her anywhere in sight.

"In here," I hear her say from the bedroom.

I walk through the living room and down the hall to the bedroom. The door is open and she's lying in bed completely naked, wearing nothing but my tie.

I smile as I walk deeper into the room, shutting the door behind me. "What's this?" I ask, already pulling my shirt over my head.

She giggles. "I have to go all weekend without touching you. I'm going to need a fix before we leave."

"Ask and you shall receive," I say, jumping onto the bed and making her squeal. My mouth lands on hers while my hips find their place between her parted legs. Her hands wrap around my waist, pulling my body down to hers.

"What time is Preston supposed to be here?" she whispers against my lips.

"We have one hour and counting."

WE WALK OUT of the bedroom only minutes before Preston walks in the front door. "Let's get this show on the road! Cal, you driving?"

I grab Piper's suitcase to take to the car. "Yeah, I'm driving."

"Great!" he cheers. "Now Pipes and I can do some booze cruising on the way. What do you say, Piper?"

"Drinking illegally while trapped on a long car ride? I think I'll pass, but feel free to drink it up in the back seat—I'm calling shotgun!"

He groans. "Man, I'm too big to ride in that little-ass back seat."

She laughs as we head toward the door. "Then be a good boy and maybe I'll trade you at the halfway point."

Preston snorts with her comment but doesn't argue. He knows as well as I do that she's serious.

The start of the drive is normal and slow. But before we even hit the halfway point, Preston gets the idea to liven things up with a game of *Would You Rather.*

"Piper, would you rather drink 20 shots of tequila or 20 shots of bear urine?"

She laughs. "What kind of question is that? Tequila, no doubt."

"But you loathe tequila," he points out.

"If it comes to drinking tequila over bear piss, I'd do it every day of the week."

I shake my head at the game they've played since we were kids.

"Preston, would you rather have to sleep with every girl you've ever done anything with, or go the rest of your life without sex of any kind?" she asks him.

"Like, I'd have to sleep with every single girl I've done *anything* with—sex, head, kissing, all of it?"

"That's right," she replies.

"That isn't fair. Some of those were nasty drunken kisses."

She shrugs. "Too bad. Screw them all or never again?"

"I don't know. I know there are a few I wouldn't touch even with

Calvin's dick. I guess no sex ever . . . No, wait. There aren't *that* many I'm ashamed of. Maybe it'd be worth it to get them out of the way first so I could enjoy the others. But *Wendy* . . . ugh. No. No sex."

"Final answer?" I laugh out.

"No sex ever again," he decides. "Calvin . . ." he starts.

"Oh, no. This is your little game," I point out.

"Fine. Piper, if you had to choose, would you rather screw Calvin or me?"

She looks nervously at me. "Calvin," she answers quickly.

"What? Why?"

She turns and looks over her shoulder at him with a smile. "Because by sleeping with you, our friendship would be over. But with Calvin, who knows what would happen? Maybe I'd fall in love and find my Prince Charming."

I shoot her a wink as Preston laughs. "You and Calvin? I don't see it working out, but whatever. It's just a game."

The game goes on a little while longer, but before I know it, Preston is passed out in the back seat.

"Shhh," Piper says, "he's finally asleep. Don't stop or he'll take my seat."

I quietly laugh. "How do you know he's asleep now and not 30 minutes ago when he finally shut up?"

"Hear that?" She points back at him and I strain to listen. "He only makes that little whimpering sound when he's really asleep."

I listen harder, and now that she's pointed it out, he does make a little whimpering sound before taking another breath. I laugh and shake my head. "I'm related to the guy. You'd think that would be something that I—not you—would know about him."

She shrugs as she reaches for her water bottle. "I've slept next to him a lot over the years. When he sleeps like that, you could probably wreck this car and not wake him."

"Good to know," I say quietly. Then, with a devious look in my eye, I lift my ass off the seat slightly. "Road head?" I whisper.

She laughs loudly and playfully smacks me across the chest.

As the trip goes on, the sun goes down. Preston wakes up right when Piper calls a padiddle.

"Why are you two playing that game? That's only a game you play when you're trying to get laid."

"We were just bored, Pres. And no, that's only a game you play when YOU want to get laid. The rest of us play it like normal-ass people."

In the rearview mirror, I see him rub his eyes. "Where are we? How much longer until we're home?"

"Just a few minutes. We're about to get off the interstate now," I answer.

"Hey, you were supposed to trade seats!" He bumps her seat, causing her to spill her water down her chin.

She laughs and wipes it dry. "I would've, but you were asleep."

"Looks like I get shotgun the whole way back then."

"What? No way!" she argues.

"Yes way. I'm calling it now."

She spins around to face him. "It doesn't work that way and you know it. You can only call shotgun as we're *getting* in the car, not three days beforehand!"

"Calvin, tell her how hard it is to scrunch your tall body into a little back seat." He tries playing me against her.

"Not doing it, dude. If it's up to me, I'm choosing her every time. She's prettier than you. And she smells better."

He shakes his head, crosses his arms over his chest, and sits back, waiting out the rest of the ride.

A little while later, the three of us are pulling into my parents' driveway. We all climb out and I pop the trunk to get our bags. Preston grabs his and starts toward the door. "See ya tomorrow, Pipes."

"I'll carry your suitcase across the street if you want," I tell her.

She smiles up at me. "Thanks."

I take my bag out and set it on the concrete to grab it on my way back. I pick up hers and walk with her across the street. At the front door, I set it down and look over my shoulder to make sure Preston isn't outside to witness our goodnight kiss.

"I'll talk to you tomorrow?" I ask, leaning in for a kiss.

"You better. Or maybe we could even manage to sneak out later tonight for a dip in the hot tub my mom finally talked my dad into buying."

"Mmm, that sounds perfect," I say, pressing my lips to hers. Her arms wrap around my neck, pulling me closer. I put my hands on the small of her back, pulling her against me. Our soft, quick kiss turns to one of passion and need—and maybe anxiousness about parting for the night. The next thing I know, I have her back pressed to the side of the house next to the front door. Her legs are wrapped around my hips and my hand is up her shirt.

"Cal, where'd you go?" Preston yells from across the street. Thanks to the darkness and the tree in her front yard, he can't see us.

I pull back. "I gotta go before we get busted. Text me later and I'll sneak over."

She smiles as I set her on her feet. Her hand is in mine and she doesn't let go until our arms can no longer stretch. Finally, we have to let go and I walk across the street.

Preston is standing on the front porch. "Where the hell have you been? They're all over me in there. Go in so they can have their golden son and leave me alone."

I laugh as I grab my bag off the ground. "Sorry, I had to carry Piper's bag across the street for her since you just ran off." I walk past him, opening the door and stepping into the foyer.

Mom squeals when she sees me, quickly wrapping me up in a big hug.

"I'm so happy to see you, Calvin. How's my boy been?"

I drop my bag. "Good, good. Where's Dad?"

She waves her hand through the air. "Oh, it's Thursday. Bowling night. Are you hungry? Have you eaten?"

"I'm starved," Preston says, stepping behind me.

"Well, come on boys. Let's get you fed."

Over a plate of spaghetti, we sit and talk and catch up with Mom. She tells us that she's been busy making all the deserts for the party this year, then goes on to list them off. She asks about the office and talks to Preston about his job. He gives vague answers and instead changes the topic to how I've somehow managed to kidnap his best friend and turn her against him.

Mom laughs at that. "Well, Calvin, what's going on with you and Piper? You know, I always thought you two would make the perfect couple."

"What the hell?" Preston says. "What about me? She's *my* friend. Why wouldn't we make the perfect couple?"

Mom rolls her icy blue eyes that match mine and my brother's. "I'm sorry, dear. I just couldn't see the two of you together. I mean, you hang out for 10 minutes and you're arguing. But Piper and Calvin," she turns to look at me, "seem to get along very well. I would always sit back and watch you have your little talks. You were always very good at calming her down, and she was good at getting you to let loose. That's what a real couple does. Each partner makes up for what the other lacks, so there's perfect balance. So, are the two of you dating?"

I snort. "What? No, Mom. We're just becoming friends again. I think she's finally starting to outgrow Preston and his childlike behavior."

He rolls his eyes and scoffs.

"Well, hopefully something will come out of it eventually. I'd like to have grandchildren while I'm still young enough to enjoy them. Keep that in mind," she says, looking at me. Then she turns to Preston and says, "You keep wrapping yours up."

"Hey!" He looks from her to me. "Why's everyone picking on me today?"

I laugh as I stand up. "Because you're a dumbass." I put my plate in the sink. "It's been a long day. I think I'm going for a shower and some sleep."

"Good night, honey."

"Night, Mom." I start to walk out of the kitchen but stop when Preston pushes his chair back.

"I think I'll call Piper and see if I can talk her into a nightcap."

I grind my teeth together but push myself forward, not wanting to stop him from hanging out with his friend.

On my way up the stairs, I shoot her a text, warning her that Preston is about to call. That way, if she wants to hang with him, she can back out of our hot tub plans. But if she wants to keep our plans, she'll have time to think up an excuse.

I'm almost up the stairs when Preston reaches for the door.

"Where you going?" I ask.

"Over to Pipes' place. What's it to you?" Without another word, he walks out and shuts the door behind him.

Fuck. He's not even going to bother to call. Looks like our plans will have to be postponed.

FOURTEEN

PIPER

I have a late dinner with my parents and spend a little time talking with them before excusing myself to my room. I'm walking up the stairs when I get a text from Calvin warning me about Preston. A few seconds later, there's a knock at the door. I turn around and walk back down the steps to answer it.

To no one's surprise, it's Preston. He flashes me that flirty smile of his. "Nightcap?" He lifts his shirt to show me the bottle of Jack tucked into his waistband like he had to sneak it out of the house.

I laugh and shake my head. "I'm tired. I think I'm just going to go to bed."

He cocks his head to the side. "All right, tell me . . . what's up with you?"

I cross my arms over my chest. "What do you mean?"

"Ever since the show, you've acted differently toward me. We're not as close as we used to be and you promised we'd still be friends—that the show wouldn't change us."

"It's not that, Pres. It's just that I'm tired. It's been a long day."

He snorts and rolls his eyes.

"Fine. Come on, we'll go out back," I tell him. He smiles wide, happy he got his way.

Calvin and I spend every evening together, so I guess I do owe Preston a night. But if this goes on too long, Calvin and I will have to cancel our hot tub date. I was really looking forward to a few minutes alone with him. But Preston is my best friend and he thinks our friendship is strained. I need to right that wrong.

Mom and Dad announce they're going to bed and ask that I lock up everything when Preston leaves. I agree to their request before walking out into the backyard. I flop down in a pool chair and he takes the one to my right. He uncaps the bottle, takes a swig, and hands it over. I do the same.

"So, what's this about?"

He shrugs. "I don't know. I just didn't want to stay there. I needed an excuse to leave, and well, you've always been my excuse," he laughs out.

"What was Calvin doing?" I take another sip and pass the bottle.

"Taking a shower and going to bed."

"Why didn't you ask him to come with? We all could've gone out or something."

"Because lately the two of you are always together and I've been feeling left out. I miss my friend, so forgive me for being greedy and wanting you to myself for one night."

I laugh and roll my eyes. "Okay, sorry. And Calvin and I aren't always together," I lie. "We just reconnected and have been becoming better friends lately. We're not leaving you out on purpose, you know."

He waves his hand through the air. "Yeah, I know. I think it's just the weirdness of that show and how I acted mixed with the growing friendship the two of you have. It makes me feel like I threw you away and he picked you up. And that isn't what I intended to do."

"I know, Pres. We're friends. We'll always be friends. You have nothing to worry about."

There's a long, drawn-out silence for a moment before he finally says, "My mom was talking about how she's always thought that you and Calvin would be the perfect couple."

"She was?" I can't help the smile that forms.

He nods. "Yeah, and honestly, it kind of pissed me off."

My brows draw together. "Why?"

"I don't know. I guess, in a way, I've always considered you mine. It just irritated me that even though you were mine, everyone always saw you with him. Like I didn't matter."

I laugh. "That isn't true. And no one ever said they saw me with Calvin."

"Your dad did that day, remember?"

"No, he said I needed to find a guy *like* Calvin."

He waves the bottle through the air. "Same thing."

I sit up and turn to face him, placing my feet on the ground between our chairs. "What's bringing all this on, Preston?"

He takes a deep breath and sits up, turning to face me. "What would you say if I told you that maybe you were right?"

"Right about what?"

"About the reason we kissed that night?"

My mouth drops open. What is he saying? "I . . . I don't . . ." I shake my head. "Are you saying you like me?"

He runs his hands through his dark hair, eyes already bloodshot from the whiskey. "I don't know. I think it's more than that. I think . . . I think I might be in love with you, Piper." Honestly is shining brightly in his eyes but he looks nervous.

I let out a nervous giggle. "I don't think so, Preston. I think you're just confused by seeing Calvin and me together so much. Maybe even a little jealous."

He shakes his head. "Maybe, but lately, I look at you and see how beautiful you are and how much you've grown up. Maybe it's time for me to grow up too. If I could do that, then we could be together, because then I wouldn't ruin this."

I stand up and take a few steps back, needing distance. "No, Preston. We could never be together. You were right. We're friends.

We'll always be friends, but we couldn't ever be more. I love you. I do. You're my best friend and I'd do anything in the world for you, but I'm not in love with you. In fact, I don't think I was in love with you when I took you on that show. I just thought I was."

I know this now because of my feelings for Calvin. I do love Calvin. I can feel it in the way my heart quickens when he gets close. I can feel it in the way my breath catches in my throat when he kisses me—the way my body fills with tingles and need and desire and passion. He makes me feel it in a way Preston never did.

He stands up and takes a step toward me. "Are you saying that if I kissed you right now, you'd push me away?"

I lick my lips and nod. "Yes. Pres, we can't go there. If you were thinking straight, you'd see that, just like you did before. Don't let my friendship with Calvin confuse you into thinking you want something you don't."

He takes another step. "You'd push me away? Let's find out." Without another word, he's directly in front of me, pulling me against his chest with his mouth on mine.

My brain doesn't have time to process what's happening. He's kissing me, but I feel nothing. I'm not even kissing him back. I have to stop this. As badly as I wanted this moment before, it's the last thing I want now. Now, I want Calvin, and no one else will ever do. Not even Preston.

I place my hand on his chest and push him back. "See? There's nothing between us. Did you feel tingles? See fireworks? Did that kiss make your heart race, your breathing pick up?" I shake my head. "It didn't for me. I think you should go, Preston." Without another word, I turn and walk back into the house, locking the glass door behind me. I look out and see him still standing by the pool where I left him. I shut off the light and walk away, heading for my room.

The moment I step inside, I text Calvin. *We need to talk.*

Preston gone?

He should be home any minute.

I toss my phone down and open my suitcase, looking for something more comfortable to put on to get out of these constricting jeans. I jump when someone taps on my second-story window. I spin around to see Calvin. I laugh as I race to the window, pulling it open.

"What are you doing? Trying to break your neck?"

He crawls inside. "It occurred to me that I'd never snuck in through a girl's window before. Wanted you to be my first." He pulls me against him and his lips land on mine. On cue, the tingles flood my body. That's why I think this is right. But right now, I have something to tell him. I pull away, taking his hand in mine. "We need to talk."

"What's going on?"

We sit on the edge of the bed, and I tell him about Preston coming over, our conversation, and how he kissed me. He doesn't get mad. There's nothing to get mad about. Preston doesn't know that Calvin and I are together. More than anything, he looks nervous.

"So Preston finally smartened up, huh?"

I shake my head. "He doesn't love me, Calvin. He's just confused. He's seen us together a lot lately. Then he had to sit and listen to your mom talk about how she's always thought we'd make the perfect couple. I think he's afraid he's going to lose me—that you're going to take me away from him."

"And what do you want?" he asks, glancing my way but trying to look impassive, like my answer won't hurt him.

I pull my brows together. "I want you, Calvin."

A knowing look spreads across his face. "You mean, you're choosing me? Preston is finally ready to give you everything you've wanted for . . . well, forever, and you're choosing me?"

I laugh and nod. "Yes, stupid. Preston is my best friend and I'll always love him. But I'm not *in* love with him. I couldn't be, because I'm in love with you."

When he hears those words leave my mouth, he pulls me against him for a kiss. It's a long, hard, fast kiss that reaches my toes and makes them go numb. He lays me back on the bed, covering my body with his, but I push against his chest, stopping him.

"We can't have sex in here, Calvin."

"What? Why not?"

"Well, for one, my parents are asleep on the other side of that wall. And two, this bed is cursed. Anyone who has sex in it will sprout hair all over their body and grow six inches."

He look confused, but I don't feel like reliving the story of my hairy uncle and his Amazon wife. "Never mind," I laugh out, shaking my head.

"How about the floor then?"

I glance down at the floor then back up to him. "Only if we're really, really quiet."

"Fine. You're the noisy one anyway," he says, sliding off the bed and onto the floor, pulling me down with him.

———

THE NEXT DAY, my mom and I are in the kitchen getting some food ready for tomorrow's party.

"Mom, I know I'm supposed to be helping, but would you mind if I invited Preston over to help?"

"Preston?" she asks, giving me a look that says, *why in the world would Preston want to cook?*

"Yeah. I feel kinda bad for him lately. He's seen Calvin and me together a lot and I think it's making him feel left out."

"Fine by me, honey," she replies, going back to her slow cooker while I dig out my phone.

I quickly type out a text to Preston: *Come over and help me cook.*

Cook? Who do you think I am? Betty Crocker?

I laugh at his stupidity. *Just come on.*

Calvin there?

Nope. It'll just be you, me, and my mom.

It's only a few minutes later when he's knocking on the patio door. I wave him in.

He opens the door and walks into the kitchen. "Good afternoon, Mrs. M."

Mom looks over her shoulder at him and offers up a smile. "Afternoon, Preston. How have you been?"

He shrugs as he sits on the barstool next to me. "Good, I guess. What are we cooking?"

"We're dicing vegetables for a veggie tray." I give him a friendly smile before handing him a knife and some broccoli.

"What are you making over there, Mrs. M?"

"I'm starting the smoked sausages for tomorrow, dear."

"Mmm, those are my favorite. Can I help her instead?" he asks me with a grin.

I jam my elbow into his ribs. "No. *Chop*."

"Why? Nobody eats the vegetable tray anyway."

"I know," I whisper. "It's literally the only job you can fuck up and no one notices. That's why I do it every year."

He nods, finally catching on. He picks up the knife and begins chopping at the broccoli, but not like a normal person. Every chop he makes is so loud, it has my mom jumping. I giggle as I place my hand on his. "Stop it before you're the one on that cutting board." I nod toward my mom. He looks up and sees her staring him down. He offers up a small smile before chopping again, this time a little more quietly.

Preston and I hang out for most of the day, which is good for our friendship, but it sucks because that means Calvin stays away. Calvin promised not to say anything to Preston about his confession and the kiss. We decided to play out this weekend as planned, then break the news to him when we get back home. That way, we can start letting our families know slowly instead of having to take them all on at once. But just because we came to an agreement on how and when to tell Preston doesn't mean Calvin is excited to fake our friendship after Preston's confession last night. Calvin's ready to tell everyone right now—officially claim me as his own.

I wouldn't mind being claimed by him, but honestly, I'm a little afraid of how Preston will take the news. Before, I wasn't sure if he'd be happy or upset by his brother and me being together. But now I'm worried because I think he already feels like he's losing me to Calvin. Telling him we're official might make those feelings worse. How can I keep my best friend and my boyfriend in my life? It seems my only option is to give Preston the time he needs to realize he's not in love with me.

After we finish helping my mom in the kitchen, Preston and I spend the rest of the day swimming and sunning by the pool. We talk, laugh, and make fun of each other like we always have. There's no mention of Calvin or Preston's feelings toward me. It's an easy day and it's one I'm happy for. Things have been so mixed up with us lately that it's nice to put it all behind us, even if it's just for now.

Preston goes back home around 7 p.m., and as I figured, Calvin shows up shortly thereafter. I pour us each a glass of wine and we sit by the pool, watching the fireflies dart above our heads. We're each in our own chairs, but they're pushed together so we can hold hands.

"How was Preston today?"

"Fine. He acted just like he always used to. I miss that Preston. We had fun. We laughed and talked and joked around. We didn't talk about anything serious. Hopefully he's realized that last night was a mistake—just a misplaced notion brought on by the feeling that he's losing me to you."

"He *is* losing you to me. You know he's going to have to accept it, right?"

"He's not losing me. I mean, sure, I'll be with you more than him now, but I'll still be there for him just like I always have been."

"Maybe that's how we should break the news to him when we get back. Just explain that even though you're with me, you'll still be his friend and will be available to talk or hang out whenever he needs. Make it clear that you won't choose between the two of us."

I squeeze his hand a little tighter. I like that. I won't choose between them. I'll keep Calvin as mine and I'll keep Preston as my best friend, and if either of them has a problem, then it'll be theirs to deal with.

I smile over at him. "I like that you put it that way."

He lifts my hand up and presses a kiss to the top.

"Will you be okay with me hanging out with him if it turns out that what he's feeling is real and doesn't fade away?" I ask.

He looks over at me. "Will you change your mind about me if you find out his feelings for you are real?"

"Absolutely not," I say, full of certainty. How I feel about Calvin is like nothing I've ever felt for anyone else, and I know that feeling can't be replaced or recreated.

"Then that'll be fine. But I better get home." He finishes up his wine and sets the glass down before standing. "It's getting late and we all know how early the fun starts around here."

I laugh as I walk him over to the gate. "Are you coming by for red, white, and blue pancakes and mimosas?"

He smiles as he pulls me closer. "You know it." My chest hits his and his lips land on mine. While he kisses me, his hands move up to cup my cheeks, keeping me against him where I like to be. The kiss is soft, slow, and long, teasing every part of me that seems to be tangled up in him forever.

———

I WAKE EARLY in the morning and take a quick shower. I decide to go for a more natural look today since I'll be in and out of the pool all day. I scrunch my hair, leaving it in soft beach waves. I don't add any makeup since it'd wash off in the water. Instead, I just apply some moisturizer. I then pull on my red, white, and blue string bikini and a pair of jean shorts. I slide my feet into some flip-flops and grab my aviator sunglasses.

By the time I get downstairs, the sound of clinking glasses is already filling the air. I walk into the kitchen to find my mom and Mrs. Young standing on either side of the island, toasting with glasses filled with orange juice and champagne. I smile as I shake my head. "Getting an early start, aren't we, Moms?"

"You know it, dear. Grab some pancakes and a flute and go enjoy breakfast with the guys." Mom motions toward the patio where my dad, Mr. Young, Preston, and Calvin are already sitting at the patio table. I grab a plate that has two pancakes, strawberry syrup, whipped cream, and blueberries. Get it—red, white, and blue pancakes? I grab a flute and hit the patio. Preston and Calvin both look up as I exit.

Calvin looks happy to see me; he's wearing a wide smile. Preston's eyes are moving up and down my body like he can't get enough of me. That look makes my skin heat up, and I immediately want to go to Calvin and give him a good morning kiss to show Preston that the way he's looking at me isn't appropriate. But I can't exactly do that.

I take the empty seat between the boys. "Looks like you guys got an early start too. Am I the only one who slept in?"

Calvin groans. "Preston made sure to wake everyone up at 7 a.m. on the dot."

I look over at him and he shrugs with a grin on his lips. "Didn't want to miss my favorite breakfast of the year."

I laugh, then dive into my pancakes. A part of me wonders if Preston was just in a hurry to get here to see me, rather than eat the pancakes. These pancakes aren't the best. I mean, strawberry syrup, whipped cream, and blueberries are fun and festive, and it's something we've done for as long as I can remember, but I don't wait all year for the pancakes. No, my favorite thing is the Independence Day punch that Mom makes. It has just about every liquor you can think of in it. It's bubbly, includes fresh fruit that only gets you more drunk if you eat it, and tastes like heaven in a glass. Every year, I get smashed off the stuff. And every year while I'm praying to the porcelain gods, I promise myself I'll never drink it again. Yet I always do.

"It's good to see you again, Piper," Mr. Young says as he sits next to my dad, across from me.

I give him my best smile. He doesn't know it, but I could be his daughter-in-law one of these days. "You too, Mr. Young. How's life been treating you?"

He nods. "As well as can be expected." He looks at my dad. "I threw my back out again last week. Took me three days, a bottle of Tylenol, and an appointment at the chiropractor to get upright." His eyes flash to Preston, Calvin, and me. "Never get old. It's hell," he laughs out, and my dad joins in.

The three of us just sit back and wonder how that could even be possible . . . I mean, unless we die, but how is that any better than getting old?

Mom and Mrs. Young come out with brand-new flutes of spiked OJ and sit in their husbands' laps. They're giggling and red-faced already. Usually, the way they get when they're drunk embarrasses me, but now I'm seeing them through different eyes. What if this is how my life turns out with Calvin? I could be sitting in his lap while Preston's at our side with his own wife. We'd all be best friends living next door to each other. Life would be like one giant party.

I let out a sigh. If only.

FIFTEEN
CALVIN

After breakfast, the music starts and the coolers are brought out. This portion of the party is only for us. Guests won't start arriving until closer to cookout time. The moms go back into the kitchen to drink, talk, and prepare food for the cookout. The dads always end up in the garage—drinking, talking about tools, and smoking weed. They've done it for years, but they'll never admit to it. It's their little tradition they think is a secret, but we all know. Preston, Piper, and I have always been left to ourselves. Back then, it was fun because we would sneak alcohol and get drunk, swim, flirt, and talk about shit we had no clue about. Then we became adults and no longer had to sneak our drinks.

It's always been fun. Except this year. I finally have Piper to myself, yet I still can't touch her. Not yet anyway. We leave tomorrow, then we can break the news. One more day. I can wait one more day.

The three of us crack open some beer and get into the pool. Piper looks amazing in that string bikini she wears every year, but it seems she fills it out a little better this year. Her chest is bigger—bouncier. Her stomach is toned, but she has a nice curve that leads to her hips.

Her ass seems rounder, but her legs are just as long as ever. I can't take my eyes off her. And neither can my brother. The way he watches her, cocks his jaw, and licks his lips has anger filling my chest. *One more day, one more day, one more day,* I keep telling myself.

Piper doesn't seem to notice as she moves around the pool on a giant floatie that looks like a pink iced donut. She has a beer in one hand, her sunglasses down, and her head back, soaking up the sun. Fuck, I just want to pull her over to the corner of the pool and slide deep inside her. If only there were a way to get Preston to leave.

"Pres, why don't you go home and grab that bottle of Fireball?"

"Fuck yeah!" he says, swimming toward the edge of the pool. He climbs out and runs for the gate.

When he's out of sight, I grab ahold of Piper's floatie and pull her closer.

"What are you doing?"

"I needed a minute alone with my girl. This bikini is sexy as fuck. I've had a boner since you walked out in it." I pull her out of her floatie and into my arms.

"What are you doing? Our parents are going to see," she says, but makes no attempts to stop me.

"Our moms are getting hammered and our dads are getting stoned. Nobody's watching us." I back her into a corner of the pool and press my mouth to hers. I can't keep my hands to myself. One hand is squeezing her breast while the other dips beneath her bikini bottom.

She giggles against my lips. "If you're going to tease me, then I'm going to tease you back, mister."

I smile. "What does that mean?"

Her hand shoots down the front of my swim trunks and latches onto my dick, which is already hard just from seeing and touching her. She slowly works her hand up and down my length. She bites her lower lip and looks up at me from beneath her lashes, letting out a soft whimper like touching me is enough to make her come.

I laugh and shake my head. "Fuck, you don't play fair."

She shoots me a grin. "I never said I did."

I can hear Preston running back toward the gate. His breathing is heavy and the liquid in the bottle is sloshing around. I quickly pull away from her, swimming away as fast as I can so he doesn't catch on.

The gate opens and he steps inside with a wide smile. "Come on, guys! Fireball time."

Fuck. I hate drinking that shit, but I knew it was the one way I could get him out of the pool to give me a few minutes alone with my girl.

Preston sets the bottle on the table and grabs three plastic shot cups. Piper climbs out to get her shot, but I'm still sporting a boner and refuse to get out.

"Come on, Cal!" Preston yells.

"I ain't getting out. Bring it to the edge of the pool."

"Who the fuck do you think I am? I ain't your server. Get out or get left out." He holds up his shot cup and Piper taps her against it. They both throw their shots back.

"I'll bring it to you, Calvin," Piper says, knowing exactly why I won't get out of the pool.

She bends down in front of me to hand me the cup, but her knees are pointed at an angle that gives me a full view of her wet-bathing-suit-covered center. It's clinging to her skin, showing me right where her slit is. It only makes me harder.

"Thank you, baby," I whisper low enough so Preston won't hear.

I take the shot and it burns all way down. I hand over the cup and she goes to pitch it. She misses the trash can and bends over to pick it up. While she's bent over with her ass pointed my way, she looks back with a smile.

Fuck. She's still playing the game and she's winning by a landslide.

It's only going on 10 a.m., and I'm already buzzed and in need of my girl. But there's no way I'll be able to get her away from Preston for any real length of time. I'm going to have blue balls by the end of the night for sure.

Hours pass and we all swim, talk, and hang out while listening to music. The moms are still in the kitchen, and the dads are still in the garage. The three of us, well, we've been doing all kinds of shit. Piper and Preston decided to have a competition to see who could do the better cannonball, with me being the judge. Preston would've won by far, but when Piper jumped in, her top came up and I saw her boobs. Obviously, she won.

The time comes when I have to get out of the pool because nature calls. I climb out and turn back to look at Piper. Her eyes are already on me and they're double their usual size. I grab my towel and start wiping off the water rolling down my chest and abs as she licks her lips. Then I look further down and see that my swim trunks are clinging to my skin the same way her bathing suit teased me. You can see every inch of my manhood. Her eyes glaze over as I give her a sexy smirk.

"Man, put that shit away!" Preston says, holding his hand up above his eyes. "What the fuck you got in there, a Maglite?"

Piper laughs out loud.

I hold up a middle finger. "You're just jealous," I tell him, walking toward the pool house to use the bathroom. Piper's eyes follow my every step until I'm no longer in view. Looks like I may have just scored a point after all.

A couple more hours pass and the moms bring out a big tray of sandwiches. After swimming all day and drinking, we're all in need of some food in our stomachs. The dads come out of the garage, load their plates down with three sandwiches apiece, plus chips and veggies, and go right back to the garage. The three of us grab sandwiches and chips and sit around the table to eat.

Eating after drinking so much usually causes one of two things to happen: you either get extremely tired and pass out, or you get your second wind—extending the party. Preston ends up in a pool chair, dead to the world. That gives Piper and me a few minutes to ourselves. With no one looking, we slip into the pool house.

"You've been a naughty girl," I tell her, pulling at the string on the back of her bikini top as she walks in ahead of me.

She giggles as she spins around to face me. "I've been naughty? You're the one walking around with that—what did Preston call it?—Maglite in your shorts."

I laugh and pull her against me. "You like my Maglite; don't pretend you don't." I untie the last strings, letting her top fall away. Her naked breasts press against my chest.

"Oh, I love your Maglite. Why don't you show me how to use it?" She grins and arches an eyebrow at me.

"I'm going to show you how to use it, all right." Without warning, I rip her bikini bottoms down her legs and pick her up against me all in one motion. Her legs wrap around my hips just as I press her back to the wall in the sitting area of the pool house. I think this pool house used to be a personal sauna, because the walls are made of sealed wooden planks. Hopefully that'll prevent anyone from hearing us.

I slide one hand between us and free myself from my shorts. We've had enough foreplay today to last us a lifetime. Pushing into her is easy. She's fucking hot as hell wrapped around my dick, and we both moan with appreciation. Our mouths meet for a fast, sloppy kiss as I move in and out of her. I pull out, thrust in, grind against her, and repeat the process. I feel her tightening around me, squeezing me with everything she has. Her breathing picks up and loud moans start to fall from her lips.

I crash mine against hers in an attempt to silence them, not wanting to get caught. I hold on to her hips to hold her in place while I push myself over the edge now that she's gotten what she needs. I thrust into her deeply and quickly, and just as my release washes over me, I hear, "What the fuck?" from behind me.

I turn to look over my shoulder, finding Preston standing in the doorway, but it's too late. My release has arrived and I can't stop it now. My hips move on their own until I've spilled every last drop inside her, too preoccupied by Preston to have the common sense to pull out.

"Preston, wait!" Piper yells just as he slams the door and marches away.

She pushes against my chest until I put her down. "I can't believe you just kept going like that, Calvin. Why didn't you stop?" she asks, pulling her bottoms back on.

I'm breathless. "I'm sorry. I couldn't stop it. Once it's there, it's coming whether I like it or not. My hips just take over. I wasn't trying to rub it in."

She rolls her green eyes and shakes her head. "I'm going after him."

"No, wait. Let me," I say, catching her hand in my own.

She looks up at me from beneath her lashes. "Are you sure you can fix this and not make it worse?"

"If I can't, then you're our only option. Let's not pull out the big guns yet." I pull her in for a quick kiss before going after Preston.

When I walk out of the pool house, all four parents are sitting on the patio. My dad looks a little proud. Hell, so does her dad. I know how much he'd rather have me with his daughter than Preston, the guy who refuses to grow up. Her mom looks a little jealous, though, and that worries me. My mom's just shaking her head, red-faced from embarrassment.

I ignore them and walk out the gate, heading for the house, where I'm sure Preston is nursing his wounds. I walk across the street and into the house. The living room is empty and so is the kitchen. I head upstairs and hear movement in his room. I knock on the door but he doesn't call out, so I open it myself and walk in to find him pulling on his T-shirt.

"Where are you going?" I ask, crossing my arms over my chest.

"Home," he answers.

"How? I drove you here," I point out.

His shoulders fall when he realizes I'm right. He shakes his head and falls into a seated position on the bed. His elbows are on his knees—his hands holding up his head as it bows forward.

"I'm sorry you found out like that," I say, leaning against the doorframe.

He looks up at me, anger painting his features. "How long has this been going on?"

I think back, wanting to answer honestly. "We first hooked up the night you went to talk to Piper after the show had aired."

"All this time?"

I shrug. "To be honest, I think we started something on your prom night. It just took a really long time to sink in."

He shakes his head, clearly annoyed. "All this time, it's been you? You were the one she was dressed all skimpy for when I showed up and ruined her hookup date? Plus that night at the restaurant when she said she was going to sue me? You were already together?"

I nod.

"Why . . . why didn't you tell me?" He stands up and starts to pace.

"I just . . . she didn't want to. We wanted to wait to make sure what we were doing was serious. We didn't want a breakup to get in the way of your friendship, or to come between our parents. After your little confession the other night, we agreed to tell you when we got back home."

"My confession? She told you about that?"

"Yep." I walk into the room and sit at the computer desk, spinning the chair around to face him.

"Man," he breathes out, falling back onto the bed, "so this is how things are going to be from now on? I tell her something personal and she goes running to tell you? I guess you stole my best friend after all, didn't you?"

I take deep breath and roll my neck to crack it and relieve stress. "It's not like that. I'm sure she only told me because you kissed her and she didn't want me to hear it from you or someone else."

"And what did she say about it?"

"She said she thinks you're feeling a little mixed up about her lately—that you think I'm trying to steal her from you and that's making you hang on to her in any way you can."

He nods. "Yeah, that's what she said to me too."

"Well, is there any truth to that?"

His fingers tie together in knots in front of him. "I'm not sure. I mean, I know I said I couldn't imagine being with her, but it felt like I was losing her. In my head, it made sense to give her what I thought she still wanted. It would've been completely selfish though. It wouldn't have been for her; it would've been for me. I figured it was the only way to keep her, so I was willing to do it."

"Just so you know, that isn't the case. I'm not making her choose me over you. I'd never do that. You're her best friend and she needs you. You're my only brother and I need you too. She and I have talked about this at length. She straight up told me she'll never choose between the two of us. So I wouldn't suggest making her try."

He looks up at me. "I wouldn't do that to her either. If you can make her happy in a way I can't, then I'm more than happy to step aside. But just so you know, whether you guys work out or not, she's always going to be in my life. She's been my best friend too long to let her go now."

I smile. "Understood. I guess I better make sure this lasts then, huh?"

He smirks as he nods. "Yeah, you better."

"Want to go back to the party?"

"Yeah, let me change and I'll be over."

I nod. "I'll wait for ya downstairs."

I leave him alone and go down to the kitchen. I grab a bottle of water out of the fridge and take a long drink, needing to rehydrate after spending all day in the sun and drinking on top of it. Preston comes down a few minutes later.

"So you're really not pissed we're together?"

He smiles and everything is right in the world. "No. I'm happy for the two of you. But seriously, the next time you two have a little secret, fill me in. That's what got me. The surprise."

I laugh as we walk out the door together. "Yeah, I'd say you walked in at a surprising moment."

He pushes me. "When someone walks in, it's common courtesy to stop thrusting, by the way."

I laugh even harder. "I couldn't help it. You caught me right in the middle of coming, man. You try stopping at that point."

He rolls his eyes and pushes me again.

"Oh yeah, that reminds me." I pull back my fist and slug him in the bicep.

He clutches it. "What the fuck was that for?"

"Because you saw my girl naked."

He laughs. "That was years ago. After seeing what I saw today, she's clearly grown. Maybe I should punch you."

"Gotta catch me first," I say, taking off running toward the gate to let myself back into the party.

When I step back in, Piper is sitting at the patio table with our parents. Fuck. We're in trouble.

SIXTEEN

PIPER

I stand back and watch Calvin chase after Preston, hoping and praying he can fix our little mistake. Once they're no longer in view, I turn to find our parents sitting at the patio table, watching me. My parents look pissed while his parents look embarrassed. Well, his mom does anyway. His dad just looks proud.

My mom reaches across the table and taps it, meaning *have a seat.*

I let out a long breath and go to sit down with them, prepared to get my ass handed to me.

"Piper, do you have something to tell your father and me?" Mom asks.

I feel my face heat up. I hate it when they ask a question they already know the answer to. "Calvin and I have been seeing each other for the last month or so."

Mom nods. "Mm-hmm, and why didn't you feel the need to tell us?"

I shrug. "We felt a new relationship had enough pressure without bringing in the family. We didn't want to break up and cause problems or awkwardness. We wanted to ensure this was going to last."

"And is it?" Calvin's mom asks.

I offer up a smile and shrug. "It seems to be. I mean, we haven't talked about the future too much, but I love him and don't see myself living without him."

"Well, I think it's great that you two are together and you're finally stopped messing around with those losers," my dad says. "Though you could've been a little quieter while the two of you were going at it like rabbits in my pool house!"

I can't help the giggle that escapes my lips, which only causes Dad to frown at me disapprovingly.

"Sorry," I say, clearing my throat.

"Given the way Preston ran out of here, I'm guessing he didn't know about the two of you either?" my mom asks.

I shake my head. "No, and I'm worried. I think he was already feeling that Calvin was trying to steal me from him. Knowing we're actually together may really push him over the edge. No matter what happens with Calvin and me, Preston is always going to be my best friend."

"Well, of course he is, honey," Mom says, placing her hand on mine and gently rubbing.

"I think Preston will come around," Mrs. Young says, offering up a smile. "It may take him some time to wrap his head around it, but in the long run, he'll be happy for his brother and his best friend."

"I hope so," I say just as the gate opens and the two of them come strolling in.

Everyone looks over at them and they freeze. Calvin finally shakes off the stares and walks over to me. He stands behind my chair and places his hands on my shoulders. "Mr. and Mrs. M, this isn't the way we wanted you to find out, but my brother has a habit of ruining things."

"Hey!" Preston says from a distance.

No one pays him any mind.

"The important thing is that Piper and I are together and we're happy. I will never hurt her, Mrs. M, and I'll always take care of her and protect her, Mr. M. Despite how we've acted today, I hope you can find it in your hearts to give us your blessing."

"Would it change anything if we didn't?" Dad asks, teasing him. But Calvin doesn't know that.

"I'd like to say *yes*, sir, but that would be a lie. I love your daughter and there's no way I could let her go. So I really hope you approve."

Dad stands up and nods toward Mr. Young. "Come with us, son."

Calvin gives me a wide-eyed look then follows along behind them. Preston tries to follow, but Mr. Young says, "No, not you. Come back when you can grow up and find the woman you want to be with."

I can't concentrate on that right now, though, because Calvin just told my parents he loves me. He hasn't even told *me* that yet! I stand up and turn in their direction.

"Calvin!" I shout, and he turns around.

I go running up to him, throwing myself in his arms. "I love you too," I whisper, leaning in to press a kiss to his lips.

He kisses me back, and I can feel the smile tugging at his lips.

"All right, you two, break it up," Dad says, pulling on Calvin's arm and forcing him to release me.

"Come on, honey. It's time to get things going for the party. Come help us in the kitchen," Mom tells me as she and Mrs. Young stand up.

"Well, can I come with you guys then?" Preston asks, making me laugh.

Mom rolls her eyes. "Come on," she agrees.

All four of us go into the kitchen and get busy taking out all the meat and veggies for the grill. Mrs. Young gets to work on making the deviled eggs while Mom gets started on the potato salad. Preston is just drunk and being stupid while the rest of us are hard at work.

"Piper!" he whisper-yells my name.

I turn to look at him and he's holding a long piece of sausage down by his groin. "Who am I?" he snickers, motioning toward the door where Calvin is.

I laugh loudly. I can't help it. I may be maturing, but I'm not so mature that I can't laugh at a good dick joke.

My mom turns to see what he's doing and she tries grabbing the sausage away from him. "Piper, your mom is grabbing my sausage!" Preston exclaims.

That only makes me laugh harder.

"Boy, let that thing go. We don't touch the meat with our bare hands," his mom tries, but again, our minds are in the gutter and we can't take anything seriously.

My mom and his mom end up stealing the sausage and chasing him out of the kitchen. They don't stop until he's diving into the pool. With my job done, I grab a frozen margarita the moms made and take it outside to get back in my donut floatie.

"Where's Calvin? He still with the dads?" I ask Preston as he floats alongside me.

He nods. "Yeah, and I smell that skunk again if you know what I mean." He smiles wide.

I feel my eyes stretch, and at the same time, we both jump off our floaties and run toward the garage. The garage door is open and all three of them are passing around a joint. Calvin takes a hit and coughs hard. His face turns beet red and his eyes water.

"Caught ya!" I yell, running through the garage.

The dads don't give a shit that they've been caught. They take a hit and pass the joint. Calvin, on the other hand, has become paranoid.

He waves the smoke away and points at the dads. "They made me do it, Piper! You know me. I don't smoke weed. EVEN IF IT IS LEGAL NOW!" When he says the last part, he leans in toward our dads, his eyes wide.

I laugh and hook my arm around his. "It's fine, but I think you've had enough." I start leading him through the garage and back toward the pool. "Thanks a lot, Dad!"

"Anytime, honey," he responds like the smartass he is.

"You want to get in the pool and cool off?" I ask Calvin.

"I think I'd drown."

"Yeah, you probably shouldn't do that. How about food? Want me to get you something to eat?"

He opens his mouth and closes it several times, making a smacking sound. "My tongue is so thick! Why is it so thick?"

I laugh as I sit him down in a chair beside the pool. "I'll get you a drink." As I walk past Preston in the pool, I point at Calvin. "Preston, watch him!"

I go inside and grab a bottle of water, then take it back outside. I find Calvin staring up at the sky, looking confused.

"What's wrong, baby?" I ask, bending down and handing him the water.

"I don't understand. It's sunny with not a cloud in sight. Where the hell is the rain coming from?"

I look up. "What rain?"

Preston busts out laughing as he holds up the Super Soaker. "This is too much fun," he says with a shit-eating grin.

Calvin sucks down the water in record time and ends up taking a little catnap in the chair. That gives me a little alone time with Preston to see what he really thinks about Calvin and me being together.

"Are you upset by the news?" I ask, bumping my shoulder against his as we sit on the side of the pool with our feet in.

"Nah. I mean, I was shocked, but after that wore off, I was actually kind of happy. I mean it. You're the best woman I've ever known, other than my mom of course. And my brother is a great guy. He's smart and hard-working. I know he'll take care of you and treat you right. I really couldn't ask for more."

I smile at his words. "And hey, maybe we'll be doing this ourselves someday. Raising our kids together just like our parents did. We could live next door or across the street from each other. Deal?"

He smiles and hooks my pinkie with his. "Deal."

The party starts to fill up with our extended family and our parents' friends. Kids take over the pool and my dad and Mr. Young hold down the grill while the moms finish up with everything inside. Uncle Peter and Aunt Beth make it to the party. They walk out onto the patio and I nudge Preston and nod toward them.

He looks up with a smile. "I couldn't even imagine those two going at it. I mean, how's it possible given that he's so short and round and she's so big and tall?"

I giggle and shrug. "No idea. You'd have to ask my bed how that worked."

"They had sex in your bed?"

"According to my mom. She promised that she changed the sheets though. Would that make you feel better?"

He snorts. "Hell no!"

"Agreed. Every time I see that bed, I get a mental image I'd rather not have."

When Uncle Paul sees me sitting on the side of the pool, he smiles and raises his hand to wave.

I force a smile, but I'm already wondering if I'm going to get kicked out of my room so they can dirty up my bed some more.

Calvin wakes just in time for the food and he's starving, putting away three plates of ribs, baked beans, potato salad, deviled eggs, and every dessert his mom brought over. After all that's done, he moves on to the Independence Day punch, replacing his high with a much more mellow buzz.

Everyone has the time of their lives like they always do at this annual party. As darkness falls, my dad and Mr. Young go out into the yard to set up the fireworks. I pull on my shorts and curl up in the chair with Calvin. He holds me close and kisses my shoulder in the darkness. Around 9:30 p.m., the first firework is lit and it explodes loudly, lighting up the sky with red, white, and blue. Each one that follows is prettier and bigger than the last.

I can't help but feel like I finally have it all. I have my best friend at my side and the love of my life with his arms wrapped around me.

"Let's sneak off," Calvin whispers into my ear.

I smile over my shoulder at him as I stand up, still holding his hand. The two of us exit the fenced-in area of the yard and walk behind it, back where the woods meet the fence. He pushes my back against the wooden privacy fence and his lips find mine while his hands find everything else. With my legs around his hips, he slides into me just as the fireworks shoot into the air and light up the sky. Even though we're on the other side of the fence where no one can see—and no one can hear thanks to the fireworks—the excitement is high just from knowing a yard full of people is on the other side of this fence.

Just as I'm about to lose all control, he whispers, "I love you."

"I love you too," I say breathily around my release.

He pounds into me until his own release rises to the surface. Quickly, he pulls out and his release hits the ground. He holds me against the fence while our hearts and bodies calm. With the fireworks going off overhead, he sets me on my feet where we both situate our clothing before walking back.

Instead of going back to the yard, I lead him up to my room. I pull him into the connected bathroom and kiss him hard while we both work on pulling off each other's clothes. He picks me up against him and steps into the shower, pressing my back against the wall as the water beats down on us. I release my legs that are wrapped around his hips and his hands come up to cup my cheeks.

I break our kiss. "Let's get cleaned up and go to bed."

After our shower, in which we took turns washing each other, we go straight to my bed. He slides his arm under my pillow and I curl into his chest. I'm out within minutes.

———

"WHAT THE FUCK?" Preston says, causing me to jump awake and see him walking into my room the next morning. "Is this how it's going to be from now on? You two always sneaking away from the party to have sex?"

I groan and turn my head into Calvin's neck to hide my eyes. "Make him go away," I beg Calvin.

"Pres, leave," Calvin says, rolling into me and wrapping me up tightly in his arms like he's trying to shield me from the weapon that is Preston.

"Sorry, big bro. No can do. It's going on 10 a.m. and we need to hit the road.

Calvin takes a deep breath. "He's right."

I groan and whine. "I'm too comfortable . . . too warm. Let's just stay here forever having sex and sleeping."

"Ugh," Preston says.

"I could live with that," Calvin replies, running his hands up and down my thighs, ass, and back. "I'll make you a deal. If you get up now and get ready, we'll stop wherever you want to have breakfast."

"No, man! You know she's going to get that stinky banana nut muffin. I need real food. Not baked goods."

I lift my head up and stick my tongue out at Preston. "Fine, I'll get up. But, um, Pres, you need to go. I'm naked under here."

Preston gives me a wide smile as he slides his hands into his pockets and leans against the dresser. "Oh, I think I'm right where I should be. I'll have the best seat in the house."

I laugh. "Well, Calvin is naked under here too. So unless you want to see his Maglite . . ." I tease.

Preston pushes up off the dresser. "See you at the car," he says, racing toward the door and leaving Calvin and me to laugh at his quick exit.

Calvin looks over at me and kisses my jaw. "I'm going to pull my clothes on and run off to pack and change into something fresh."

"I'll meet you there," I agree, leaning back on the bed and watching his glorious body as he puts on his clothes.

I pull on a pair of black running shorts, a sports bra, and a tank top.

I slide my feet into a pair of flip-flops, just wanting to be comfortable for the long ride home. I pull my hair up into a high ponytail and throw everything into my suitcase before making my bed and leaving the room. I drop my things by the door and head into the kitchen where Mom and Dad are both sitting at the table, looking tired and hung over.

I motion toward the Youngs' home. "The boys are ready to go."

Mom nods. "Okay, dear. Safe travels." She stands up slowly to give me a hug. "I'm getting too old for these Fourth of July parties. You need to hurry up and get married so we can pass it down to you."

I smile. "But you do it so well. And don't hold your breath on me getting married. I love you." I kiss the top of her head before pulling away and heading for the door.

I walk across the street and find Preston leaning against the car. Calvin's just walking out. He's wearing a pair of khaki shorts with a blue fitted T-shirt. Just seeing him has me licking my lips. He smiles when he sees me and holds out his arm for my suitcase.

"You're looking sexy in those shorts, babe," he says as he leans in for a kiss.

I laugh. "You're sweet, but I look like crap and feel even worse. That damn punch gets me every year! How are you feeling?"

Calvin shrugs. "I feel great."

Preston pushes himself up off the car. "I'd feel great if I'd taken a three-hour nap yesterday too."

I snort. "You didn't get stoned, Preston," I point out. "Why did you smoke anyway?" I ask Calvin as he loads our things into the trunk.

"It felt like some kind of welcome into their club. I couldn't turn it down. But fuck, I wish I had. I was so stoned I thought I felt my hair growing."

I laugh. "You also wondered why your tongue was so thick and how it could be raining on you when it was sunny."

Preston laughs.

Calvin shakes his head. "I'm never smoking weed again."

The three of us pile into the car with Preston volunteering to sit in the back now that he knows Calvin and I are a thing. Once we get on the road, Calvin reaches over and holds my hand. I love these little things I didn't even notice were missing before. But finally having this secret out feels great. There's no more hiding or lying or having to act differently when my best friend comes around. Calvin and I can finally be totally together now and I can't wait to see where we end up.

SEVENTEEN

CALVIN—ONE MONTH LATER

"I can't believe my brother and best friend are going to Hawaii for a whole week and I don't get to go," Preston whines as he throws himself down on my couch while I double-check our hotel room reservation.

"It's our first trip as a couple. Would you want your little brother going?"

"If he were as cool as me? Yeah!"

I roll my eyes.

"Can't I come, please? I promise I'll leave you guys alone."

"No, Preston. I have something very important to do on this trip and you cannot come."

He looks at me with annoyance written on his face. "It's a vacation. What could you possibly have to do?"

I give him a smile before pulling a small black box out of my pocket. I open it and show him the ring. "You think she'll like it?"

His mouth drops open as his eyes take in the large diamond. He leans forward and takes the box to inspect it closely. "Like it? She's going to love it!"

I smile as I take the box and put it back in my pocket to resume confirming our reservations.

"I can't believe my best friend and brother are going to get married."

"Don't jinx me. I haven't asked her yet. She could still say no."

He snorts. "She's not saying no. You've ruined her with that Maglite of yours. She couldn't be with anyone else if she wanted to!"

I reach over and slug him in the shoulder. "Fuck off." I take a deep breath. "But seriously, you think she'll say yes?"

He looks at me seriously now and says, "She's going to say yes, man." I can see the honestly shining in his eyes.

"And how do you feel about that? I know us getting together was a little hard to swallow at first."

He waves his hand through the air. "Piper was right, of course. I was just feeling lost, I guess. She hadn't been around much and I was feeling lonely. But now that you're keeping her off my back, I've had a lot of time on my hands. I've been dating a few different girls."

"Yeah, any of them going to stick?"

"There's one I really like. She reminds me of Piper a lot. She's funny and gets these wild ideas in her head. Plus she's adventurous and playful. Hopefully things work out."

"Good. I'm glad to see you moving on." All of our reservations seem to be in order, so I close the browser and stand up. "Time to pack."

"Does Piper know where you're going?"

"Of course she does. She's packing now."

"But she has no idea you're going to propose?"

I laugh. "No, and don't spoil it by telling her. I want it to be a surprise. I have the whole thing set up. Our room has a balcony that overlooks the beach. I have a romantic dinner planned for tomorrow night. Right when the sun goes down, I'm going to get on one knee and ask her."

"So you're asking her on the first night?"

"Yeah, why?"

He shrugs. "What if she says no? That will ruin the rest of the trip, won't it?"

I offer up a grin. "She won't say no. I'm asking her at the beginning so we can spend the rest of the trip tangled up in each other."

He shakes his head. "I can't wait until the doing-it-all-the-time phase ends for you guys. I've seen you two fucking more than I've watched porn this month."

"Well, knock before you walk into a damn room and that won't happen again."

"I would if I were walking into a bedroom. You don't think to knock before walking into a fucking kitchen!"

"You should if it's not your kitchen!" I point out.

"It wouldn't be bad if I walked in and saw Piper, but no, I always walk in to see your fucking ass."

I laugh. "Yeah, I always make sure she's pointed away from the doorway. You're welcome."

He holds up his middle finger.

Preston helps me get everything down to my car and we both make the drive over to Piper's. He's going to ride with us to the airport and drive my car back home so it doesn't have to sit in the parking lot for a week. We walk into Piper's place and she's nowhere near ready. There are clothes thrown all over the bedroom, her suitcase is open on the bed, and she's running from room to room like a chicken with its head cut off.

I grab ahold of her wrist and pull her to my chest. I cup her face with my hands as I look into her eyes. "Calm down. It's just a trip. Whatever you forget, we can buy when we get there." I close the distance between our lips.

She nods with her eyes still closed from our kiss. "I know. You're right."

Our flight isn't until 2 a.m., so we have plenty of time to get her packed up since departure isn't for another five hours. I walk into the living room to find Preston on the phone, ordering a pizza.

"Good idea. Get cheesy bread," I tell him, knowing Piper will never forgive me if I don't add it on.

Preston rolls his eyes but adds it to the order. Piper finally hauls out her suitcase and leaves it by the door. I take a moment to look her up and down. She's wearing a pair of sweatpants that hug her hips and ass nicely. She's wearing a pair of Ugg boots and a baggy sweatshirt. Her honey-blonde hair is piled high on her head in a messy bun, and she has a dark pair of sunglasses up there as well. It's clear she's going more for comfort than fashion on this late-night trip. But even in baggy sweats, she still steals the breath from my lungs.

She comes and sits down on my lap, wrapping her arms around my neck.

"Preston ordered some pizza and cheesy bread," I tell her.

"Yum, good. I'm starving."

"Me too," I whisper in her ear.

Preston didn't hear, but his head whips around and he gives me that don't-even-think-about-it look. I shoot him a smile as he rolls his eyes and shakes his head.

The three of us sit on the couch and watch TV while we wait for our food. It's finally delivered and we kick back to eat while watching an episode of *Reveal Your Secret*. I can't help the smile that forms on my lips. This is what got us to where we are now. And this episode is even better, because they used a scene from Piper and Preston's show in their introduction.

"I can't believe they did that!" she says, mouth hanging open.

I laugh and Preston shoots her a glare. "I'll never forgive you for taking me on that shit show."

She laughs. "You know you already have. Plus imagine the stories we'll be able to tell our future kids about our weird little threesome relationship. Wait . . . on second thought, I don't think we should call it that."

"We definitely shouldn't call it that," I agree. "Any threesomes we have will not include my brother."

"Oh, come on. You got your chance to bump uglies with Pipes. When's my turn?" Preston asks.

Piper giggles but drills him in the thigh with a solid punch.

"Dammit, I'm going to be black and blue by the time I leave the two of you. Did you know that Calvin punched me just because I saw you naked before he did?" Preston rats me out.

Piper looks from him, to me, and back. "Yeah, he said he was going to do that."

Preston's mouth drops open. "And you let him?"

She shrugs as she takes a big bite of cheesy bread. "I mean, it only seemed fair."

"How in the hell is that fair? Maybe if he hadn't been such a stick-in-the-mud growing up, you two would've hooked up a long time ago instead of you wasting all that time chasing after me."

She knocks her elbow against his. "Everything worked out just the way it was supposed to, Pres." She leans into me and I kiss the top of her head, thankful that she was finally able to see me and the love I have for her in spite of her screwed-up relationship with my brother. I don't know what I would've done if that show had gone any differently. I thank God every day for finally nudging her toward me.

When the time comes, we all load up in the car and make the drive to the airport. I give Preston a hug before he runs off. "Thank you . . . for everything. I have a feeling that this is all because of you."

He looks at me, confused. "What do you mean?"

"I mean, if you were any smarter, you would've snatched Piper up before I even saw her. But luckily for me, you're a dumbass and she's all mine." I offer him a wide grin and he holds up his middle finger behind Piper's back as he hugs her.

"Remember, Pipes, if you get pissed off at my brother on this trip, just kick him in his Maglite." He shoots me a smile.

"No way, I love that Maglite . . . until it's going down my throat, that is."

Preston fakes a vomiting sound from too much detail.

She points at him with a smile. "That's exactly what I sound like!"

I laugh and he shakes his head. "Get out of here before you make me sick."

I hold out my hand and she takes it, allowing me to lead her through the airport and onto the plane, where we sit in first class. She sits down, puts on her seatbelt, and pulls her legs up to turn toward me. "This is going to be so much fun."

"You have no idea," I tell her, placing my finger under her chin and directing her in for a kiss. She kisses me softly and slowly, but even that's enough to have me ready to pull her ass back to the bathroom to join the Mile High Club.

When the plane takes off, she puts on an eye mask and rests her head on my shoulder, ready to sleep the flight away. While she sleeps, I can't do anything but watch her. I'm so fucking caught up in her that I can't think of anything but putting that ring on her finger and making her mine for the rest of our lives.

———

WHEN WE GET TO HAWAII, we go to our hotel and decide to take a little nap before we start our day. She kicks off her boots, lets down her hair, and removes her sunglasses before climbing beneath the blankets. I kick off my shoes and strip out of my shirt and shorts before crawling up behind her. I pull her close to my chest and the two of us are out within minutes.

When we wake, we decide to spend our first day lounging on the beach. The two of us strip down to our swimsuits and head out, finding a couple of chairs under a big palm tree. The waiter comes over and I order the hotel's signature drink. Piper decides to hold off a little while longer since we haven't had a full meal in a while. She orders some sparkling water instead.

"Do you want to get something to eat?" I ask, reaching over to run my fingers down the soft skin of her cheek.

"Didn't you say you already had dinner plans set up?"

"I did," I agree.

"Well, that's fine. I'll just wait and eat then. If I eat now, I won't be hungry for dinner."

"Do you want a snack or something? I saw a little snack bar up there and could grab you something. We still have a few hours before dinner."

"I'll be fine," she promises, offering me a smile before turning her attention back to the ocean. "This place is beautiful. I could stay right here in this chair with you forever."

I pick up her hand and press a kiss to the top. "Me too, Piper. Me too."

We spend the day enjoying the beach, resting, and getting some sun. When it gets close to dinnertime, we make our way back up to our room to shower and dress. I shower first so I have time to get everything set up while she gets ready. The balcony has a big table in the center with two white candles burning. There's a bottle of wine already chilling and breathing, and I ordered our favorite dinners.

She walks onto the balcony while the sun is still in the sky, starting its slow decline. I look up and I'm breathless. She's wearing a white summer dress. It's thin and flowing around her with the light breeze. The dress is long and covers her legs, but her arms are left bare, showing off the sun she got on her shoulders and collarbone today. I walk over and take her hand in mine, bringing it to my lips, where I press a soft kiss against it.

"You're absolutely breathtaking."

Her cheeks turn a slight shade of pink as I lead her over to the table and pull out her chair for her. She sits down and I scoot it up, taking my seat across from her.

I grab the bottle of wine and pour some in both glasses. "I know we talked about this vacation over a month ago, but there was actually another reason I wanted to take it."

"To get Preston out of the way?" she jokes.

I laugh as I shake my head. "Well, that too." I stand and move to the side of the table, falling to one knee. I reach into my pocket and pull out the box, opening it to show her the ring. "Piper, I know we haven't been together all that long yet, but already I know you're the only one I want. I want to make you mine in every way possible. I want the pleasure of going to bed with you every evening and I want to wake up next to you every morning. I can't wait another day to start my future with you. Will you marry me?"

Her eyes are wide with surprise and they're slowly filling with tears. She's smiling when she nods. "Yes! Yes, I'll marry you, Calvin."

Finally, I can breathe out a sigh of relief. I take the ring out of the box and slide it onto her finger, pulling her against me in the same second. I kiss her like it's the last time I'll ever get to kiss her. Already, dinner is forgotten as I pick her up and lay her down on the balcony lounge chair. My hips push her legs apart as I press my body against hers.

As we kiss, my hands move her dress up until I can hook my fingers around her panties and yank them down. I reach between the two of us to free myself from my shorts, but her hand moves up to cup my jaw.

"Calvin, there's something I have to tell you first."

My hands freeze as I stare down at her.

"I'm pregnant," she whispers around a smile.

Did I hear her correctly? "Did you just say that you're pregnant?"

She nods. "I just found out. I'm not that far along yet."

"How?" I ask, trying to figure out how and when. We've always used condoms or I've pulled out. I mean, I know the pull-out method isn't foolproof, even with her being on birth control, but I was pretty damn sure I always did it in time.

"The pool house," she says, and suddenly I remember. Preston walked in and distracted me. It was the only time I didn't pull out. "Are you upset?" she asks. "I know it wasn't planned." She suddenly seems worried.

I laugh. "No, I'm not upset. This is awesome. We're going to be parents!" I lean in and press my mouth against hers. Our excited kiss turns to one of need and I find myself right where I left off. I free myself from my shorts and push up into her, connecting us as one like we were made to do. I hold her tightly as I thrust into her, making her call out with every rock of my hips. She digs her nails into my back— only making me work harder. With one last roll of my hips, we both come undone together and I know I'll never be the same again.

EIGHTEEN

PIPER

Calvin and I enjoy every minute of our tropical vacation even though I can't drink. We lie on the beach, catching some rays. We swim and play in the water. We eat delicious food, dance, cuddle, kiss, and talk about our future now that we're engaged to be married and have a baby on the way.

A part of me wants to go back home and tell everyone the news about the baby, but it's all too soon. Calvin and I have agreed to go home and tell everyone about the engagement, then start planning a small winter wedding before I show too much. After the wedding, once the pregnancy is farther along, we'll break the news to the family.

Preston is there to pick us up from the airport like promised. He's wearing a big smile like he already knows what happened on our trip. I take off running toward him and jump into his arms. He catches me and spins me in a circle.

"Have a good time?"

"The best," I say as he places me on my feet. I hold up my hand. "Looks like we're going to be related."

He laughs. "Damn, I was hoping you'd tell him no so we could run off together."

"Yeah, right," Calvin says, putting an arm around my shoulders.

"So, when's the wedding?" Preston asks, handing Calvin the keys.

"We're thinking this winter. A church wedding back home with close friends and family. Then the reception in the grand room at the country club." I climb into the passenger seat and Preston slides into the back.

"This winter? Why so soon? Don't you guys want to test the waters a bit before just jumping in?"

I roll my eyes. "No way. I know what I'm getting myself into. I'm ready to jump in with both feet."

Calvin looks over at me and gives me a breathtaking smile. "Me too."

"So, where are you guys going to live?"

"Calvin and I have talked about it, and it seems to make more sense to sell his place and live in mine . . . at least for the time being. We might decide to move back home when we start our family. You know, the city is no place to raise a big family, and that's what we want. I'm thinking at least five little ones."

Preston's eyes nearly bug out of his head. "Five? You want *five* kids? Holy hell, Piper. Those little shits will be walking out of there by the end of it. Then again, with Calvin's Maglite, even the first one might walk out," he jokes.

Calvin holds up his middle finger and I reach behind my seat, swinging blindly at Preston. I never land a hit, so he keeps laughing.

"We're getting started on the plan, so you need to hurry and catch up," I tell him.

"What are you talking about?" Preston asks.

I spin in my seat to look at him. "We agreed that we'd live next to each other and raise our kids together, so our kids can have a childhood like we did. You'd better hurry up and find the one you're going to marry!"

He rolls his eyes. "Ugh, I'm going to need a little more time. If you buy a house, just make sure there's one next door for me."

Since it's not possible to go back home right now to tell our parents about the engagement, we settle for video chatting with them instead. As soon as we unpack, clean up, and settle in, he calls his parents from his phone.

"What the hell is this shit?" his dad asks, flipping the phone in different directions trying to figure out the video call. He puts it up to his ear. "Hello?"

"Dad, look at the screen," Calvin says, making us both giggle.

He pulls the phone away from his ear and looks at the screen. Calvin raises his hand and waves. "It's a video call, Dad."

"What the hell is a video call?"

"It's exactly like it sounds. Where's Mom?"

"Oh, she's in the kitchen cooking something."

"Can you go to her? We have something we want to tell both of you."

"Well, all right," he says, moving the phone all around to get up out of his recliner.

After a minute, they're both on the screen.

"Oh, it's Calvin and Piper. What are you two up to?" his mom asks.

"Well, we just got back from our vacation in Hawaii, and we wanted to call and tell you that . . ."

"We're engaged!" we both say at the same time as I hold up my hand and show them the ring.

His mom giggles and jumps and squeals and cries. To say she's excited is an understatement. His dad smiles, gives him a head nod, and says, "Congratulations, Son."

"Thanks, Dad."

"Does Preston know yet?" his mom asks, sounding a little worried.

"Yeah, he knows and he's happy for us," Calvin replies.

"Well, good. How did your mom take the news, Piper?"

"Uh, we actually haven't told her yet. We're calling them next."

"We're the first?" This makes her start crying again. She wants to know everything: What's the date? Which location did we choose? Why so soon? When are we going to start having kids and making her a grandma? She peppers us with question after question until we finally have to end the call to share the news with my parents.

I call my dad from my phone and he answers, "What's up, Pipes?"

"Where's Mom? We want to talk to you both."

"She's knitting," he says, sounding confused.

"Knitting? When did she start that?" I ask, trying to remember if I've ever seen my mom knit.

He shrugs as he gets up from his seat in the living room. "It's the damnedest thing. She took up knitting when she was pregnant with Jake. Then she stopped and didn't start again until she was pregnant with you. Then she stopped again and hasn't touched the knitting needles for, well, 25 years. The other day, she just picked them up and has been knitting ever since."

My jaw drops. "Dad, did you knock up my mother?" I almost yell.

"Motherfucker better not have," he mumbles as he walks into the bedroom where my mom is.

She smiles at the phone. "Hi, honey."

"Hey, Mom. Did Dad knock you up again?"

Her eye stretch wide. "What? Good Lord, no! I can't get pregnant anymore. I'm too old for that nonsense."

"So what's with the knitting?"

She shrugs. "I was cleaning out the attic and came across it. It just seemed like something to do to keep my hands busy."

I nod, wondering if she somehow knows about my pregnancy even if she doesn't actually know. Mother's intuition? "Well, Calvin and I just got back from Hawaii . . . and guess what?"

"What?" she asks, looking excited.

"We're engaged!" I say, holding up my hand to show her the ring.

THE WRONG BROTHER   169

"Well, that's wonderful, honey." My mom is a lot more chill than Calvin's mom, but get them together and they act like teenagers. "When's the big day?"

"Late fall or early winter. We're thinking end of November or beginning of December. Whatever the church has available."

Her smile widens. "You're getting married at home?"

I look at Calvin then back at her. "We both thought it would be better to go back home. You know, it's where everything started for us."

Calvin reaches behind me and pulls me closer, his hand rubbing up and down my back. He presses a kiss to the top of my head.

"And have the two of you thought this through? You haven't been together for very long," Dad points out.

"We wouldn't have it any other way, Dad."

Calvin and I talk to my parents a little while longer before hanging up. I lie back on the couch and place my hands on my flat tummy. I can't wait until it starts to expand and I can actually see how much our baby is growing.

Calvin is sitting at the end of the couch and he leans over to place both of his hands on my stomach, next to mine.

"Are you happy?" he asks, looking into my eyes.

I smile and nod. "Are you?"

"Never been happier," he replies as he works his way up my body to kiss my stomach. He keeps one hand on it and lightly lays his head next to his hand. "We can't wait to meet you, little one," he says to the baby.

I laugh. "I don't think it has ears yet, Calvin."

He shrugs. "So it might not be able to hear yet, but it can feel love. And love makes everything grow bigger and stronger." He offers me up a smile and kisses my belly again.

The front door opens and Preston walks through. He walks right by us on the couch, heading for the kitchen. Calvin and I both hold our breath, hoping he doesn't realize what we're doing.

Preston doesn't make it to the fridge though. He stops dead in his tracks and walks backward until he can clearly see the two of us. He pulls his brows together and squints at us. "What are you doing?"

"Just relaxing," I answer.

"Not you," he says to me as he turns his head a little more toward Calvin. "*You*. What are you doing?"

Calvin looks like a deer in the headlights. He's between my legs with his head at my stomach. "I . . . was about to go down on her. Why else would I be here?"

My face heats up and nearly burns from embarrassment. I smack Calvin's arm and he sits up. "What?" he asks, giving me that look that says, *I panicked and didn't want to tell him the truth.*

Preston gives us his side eye but lets it go as he heads into the kitchen.

"Why would you say that?" I whisper at Calvin now that we have a few seconds alone.

He shrugs. "I panicked. I couldn't exactly tell him the truth."

Preston is back with three beers. He hands one to Calvin and one to me. I look at the bottle in my hands and set it on the coffee table.

"What's wrong?" Preston asks, noticing I didn't open my beer.

"I just don't feel good. I'm tired and have to work in the morning. You two go ahead."

"It's just one beer, Pipes. I highly doubt one beer is going to give you a hangover," Preston tries.

I shrug. "I drank way too much on our little vacation. I'm just not feeling it tonight. What are you doing here? I figured you'd be sick of us by now."

He smiles but takes a sip of his beer to cover it up. "I missed you guys. Tell me what you did in Hawaii. Did you go parasailing like we talked about?"

"No," Calvin and I both say together.

"Well, did you do the rock climbing?"

"No," we both say in unison again.

"Did you go on that deep cave dive I found online?" He looks so hopeful.

We both shake our heads.

Preston is now annoyed. "So, what did you do?"

I smile wide and Calvin says, "Well, we spent a lot of time in our room." And I can't help the giggle that escapes.

Preston shakes his head. "You guys can have sex anywhere. Why waste a trip to Hawaii?"

"Exactly. We can do it anywhere and we're going to do it everywhere," Calvin laughs out.

Preston shakes his head. "You two better be careful or you'll end up pregnant."

Calvin and I look at each other, then at Preston. Preston looks at me, then at his brother, and back. I see Preston's eyes travel from mine, to my breasts, and then to my stomach.

"Aw, man. You already are, aren't you?" he asks, running his hand through his thick, dark hair.

"What? No! I'm not pregnant," I lie.

He rolls his eyes. "It's written all over your faces. Calvin looks happy for no reason," he points out.

"I have a reason to be happy. We're getting married," he argues.

"Yeah, but that's a kind of happy that only lasts the day or when it's brought up. Not constantly. And you, Piper—you're glowing. Your face is lit up and your eyes are sparkling. And it looks like your boobs are already a little firmer. You're pregnant, aren't you? I noticed your boobs before you guys even left. I just thought you bought one of those Victoria's Secret bras or something, but now it all makes sense. I bet it was the pool house, wasn't it?"

I can't keep this secret any longer. Not from my best friend. "Yes," I breathe out.

Preston looks proud of himself for figuring it out, but that look is quickly replaced with disgust. "Man, I witnessed my niece or nephew being made? Gross, man." He shuts his eyes and massages his temples, causing us to laugh.

"No one knows yet, and we're not telling everyone until after we're married. So you have to keep this secret. Got it?" I point at him.

"I guess we have you to thank, Preston. If you hadn't walked in and distracted me, I would've been able to pull out in time." Calvin smiles over at him.

"You're welcome, I guess," Preston says, finishing off his beer.

"Oh, and Pres . . ." I say, sitting up and turning to face him. "We've talked about it and in addition to being this baby's uncle, would you also like to be the godfather?"

This surprises him. He sits up a little taller. "Well, who's going to be the godmother?"

"We were thinking of asking my friend Riley."

"So the godfather and the godmother get to hook up, right?" He smiles wide.

My jaw drops. "What? No, you freak!"

"Why not?"

I shake my head. "Never mind."

He laughs. "I'd be more than happy to be godfather to your child, but I will show you that the godfather and godmother *do* get to hook up."

"Leave my friend alone, Preston," I say, leaning forward and pointing my finger at him.

But he doesn't take me seriously. Instead, he only laughs harder.

"I can't believe my whole life I've been the screw-up and Calvin's been the golden child, and now he's the one having the shotgun wedding," Preston laughs. "I can just see Mr. M standing at the altar with you two, holding the shotgun on you, Cal." He laughs some more. "I mean, seriously, if you'd asked our parents which one of us they thought would knock a girl up and have to marry her, 10 to one, they would've said me."

Calvin holds up his middle finger. "Yeah, but it's not like Piper and I were just fucking around. If *you* knock someone up, it's going to be some woman whose last name you don't know."

Preston looks pissed for being called out. He doesn't respond though. He just grabs his phone and starts typing. A few seconds later, "White Wedding" by Billy Idol starts playing.

Calvin picks up a couch pillow and chucks it at Preston's head. His head goes flying back from the force of the pillow, but Preston just holds up his middle finger and smiles.

"Hey, I know what we can do. Let's pick out the wedding playlist. We could make CDs—I know, *so* retro—and hand them out at the wedding as party favors. We'll start with 'White Wedding,' and after that, we'll switch gears to 'Papa Don't Preach' by Madonna." He looks up from his phone and flashes me a grin.

I can't do anything but laugh as I shake my head at how stupid he is.

———

TIME PASSES by in a blur as we chug along to our wedding day. There's a lot of traveling back home to set things up for the wedding. Calvin manages to sell his penthouse. It takes us almost a week, but we finally get all of his things moved into my place—*our* place.

We start working on the room that will soon belong to our baby. Even though we don't know the sex yet, I wanted to get a jump on things. I picked out a beautiful cream-colored carpet and painted the walls a soft yellow with white trim. We've both been buried in work and I had a doctor's appointment where we got our first sonogram picture. I was only eight weeks along at the time, so I'm not able to make out much in the picture, but I love it anyway because I know it's a product of the love Calvin and I have for each other. I get a frame for the picture and place it on a shelf in the baby's room, next to a picture of Calvin and me that I had framed. Above the shelf, it reads *All Because Two People Fell in Love*.

The pregnancy is still a secret where our families are concerned, even though morning sickness is hitting hard. We spent last weekend at home while we reserved the church and the great room for the reception, and the entire time I had to come up with excuses to run to the restroom and empty my stomach. But Calvin was great at covering for me and choosing things in my absence.

I've never been the type of girl who fantasized about her wedding day, so every choice I make is like shooting in the dark. But my mom and Calvin's mom are always there to help. They even volunteered to plan the whole thing since I'm far away and buried in work. I almost took them up on their offer, but decided that this wedding is about Calvin and me. We should be the ones to plan it and represent our love. I did give them a few tasks to handle on their own, though, like sending out invites to family, keeping the church up-to-date on any changes, and managing the families.

Calvin and I have decided not to register for any gifts considering we have everything we need. We actually have twice as much as we need since we combined two homes into one. Most of his things are in storage or in boxes in my garage. Despite all the stress I'm under with work, the wedding, and the baby, I'm unbelievably happy and never pictured my life going this way. I love that when I get home from work, he's already preparing dinner. I love falling asleep in his arms every night and waking up to him bringing me a hot cup of coffee every morning. I even love the little things like seeing his shaving kit on the bathroom counter, his car in my garage, and his favorite coffee cup sitting next to mine. I love that I've finally found my other half and feel like kicking myself most days for not truly seeing him sooner. Calvin is absolutely perfect for me in every way, shape, and form. In fact, I think I need to punch Preston for standing in our way for so long. Plus, it would help to let out some of this stress.

Now that Calvin and I are living together, Preston seems to be around that much more. He's at our house every day, and we have dinner with him most nights. Honestly, I'm surprised he hasn't tried climbing into bed with us yet. It's like we're all one big, happy family and I wouldn't have it any other way.

This evening we have a dinner planned to tell Riley about the pregnancy. I'm also going to ask her to be the godmother. We weren't planning on inviting Preston, since we knew he'd suggest that they sleep together as part of their duties as godparents, but he overheard us talking about it and invited himself.

The doorbell rings at 5 p.m., and I know it's Riley because Preston would've just walked in. I answer the door and she pulls me in for a hug.

"Where's the wine?"

I laugh as I hug her back. "It's already being chilled," I promise.

I walk her into the house and out to the patio where Calvin is standing at the grill.

"Riley, this is Calvin, my fiancé. And honey, this is my friend Riley."

They shake each other's hands and have a moment of chitchat before Preston makes his presence known—striding onto the patio with an open beer in his hand. He looks Riley up and down. "Who's this?"

"Preston, this is Riley. Riley, Preston. He's Calvin's brother and my best friend since kindergarten."

She holds out her hand to shake. "It's nice to finally meet the man who broke my best friend's heart on national television." She knows everything worked out for the best, but she just wants to put him on the spot.

Preston's mouth drops open and his eyes move from her, to me, and then to Calvin. For the first time in his life, he's speechless. "Umm, I . . ."

She bursts out laughing. "I'm just joshing ya. Relax."

He lets out a nervous laugh and goes to sit at the patio table.

We all take our seats and Calvin reaches over to hold my hand. "Riley, we actually have something to tell you," I start.

"Wow, this feels very formal. And all without a drink in my hand."

Preston pulls a beer out of his pocket and hands it over.

She laughs. "Thanks." She pops it open and takes a sip.

"As you know, Calvin and I are getting married this winter."

She nods.

"Well, the reason we're having the wedding so soon is because I'm pregnant!"

Her eyes double in size and her mouth drops open, the corners turning up slightly. "What? Seriously?"

I smile and nod. "And since you and I are so close, I was wondering if you would consider being the baby's godmother."

She seems surprised and taken aback. "Godmother? That's a thing?"

I shrug one shoulder. "I mean, it's mostly just a promise to help guide the baby when he or she needs it. Be a parent without all the responsibilities."

"Oh. And who's the godfather?" she asks.

Preston smiles wide and holds up his hand. "It's going to be you and me, baby." He winks at her and I can't hold back my laugh.

"That in no way, shape, or form means you two get to have sex," I point out, just to remind him again.

"What?" she asks.

I wave off her question. "Preston is stupid and thought that him being the godfather was a free pass to try out the godmother."

"I'm still down to try," he says, wagging his bows and nodding his head while his eyes stay locked on her. He looks more creepy than anything.

"Riley, I'm sorry my brother is such a dumbass," Calvin says, glaring at Preston. I can tell he's afraid that Preston's going to mess this up for us.

Riley laughs. "Yes, I'll be the godmother!"

"You will?" I ask, wondering if she knows what she's gotten herself into.

She nods. "Yes! How could I pass up being a member of this family?"

I stand up and pull her in for a hug. "Thank you so much. And don't worry about Preston. We all just beat the shit out of him whenever he needs it. Now that you're in the family, you have that right too." I smile over at him.

"Hey!" he says, frowning in my direction.

NINETEEN

CALVIN—THREE MONTHS LATER

"Are you ready for this?" Piper asks me as we pack our bags to go back home for the wedding.

I'm holding my phone charger and toss it into my bag that's sitting on the bed as I turn to face her. She's only a foot away from me, so I pull her against my chest, then spin us around so I can lay her back on the bed, careful to keep my weight off her belly. "I've never been more sure of anything in my entire life."

She smiles and it seems like all her nervousness falls away.

"I think the real question is: Are *you* sure?"

She frowns. "Why wouldn't I be sure?"

I shrug as I lie at her side. "I don't know. I just don't want to have some kind of runaway bride situation on my hands. You know, me standing up at the altar waiting for a bride who's suddenly run off with my brother," I joke.

She laughs. "You think I'd run off with Preston?"

"No, I'm just saying that if you *were* to run away, you'd probably take your best friend with you."

She wets her lips as her eyes take in my face, starting at my eyes and falling down to my lips. "There's no place on earth I'd rather be than with you, Calvin." She lifts her head and presses her soft lips to mine.

As I kiss her deeply, I place my hand on her stomach, holding our child. Piper's so thin that I can notice even the smallest bulge. She doesn't look pregnant though. If anything, she looks like she's gained a few pounds, which could be written off given the stress of planning a wedding. She's already become self-conscious about it, though, so outside the house, she's opted to wear loose-fitting tops. She's afraid someone will notice her stomach and think she's either pregnant or fat. I'm just glad we'll finally get to tell our families about the baby at the reception this weekend.

We've talked about how to tell them over the last few months. We thought telling everyone over the toasts would be a good idea, but you know Piper—everything has to be a grand gesture. After mulling over several ideas, we finally figured out the perfect way to tell them . . . though I wonder if they'll catch on.

"Let's hit the road," I say, pulling away and helping her to her feet.

The drive is long and with her growing belly comes more bathroom stops than I'm used to. All the stopping to pee, eat, and stretch her legs because of a cramp almost doubles the drive time, but we finally make it.

The wedding is tomorrow, so we've agreed that she will stay with her parents tonight and I'll stay with mine. Then after the wedding and reception, Preston will take us to the airport for our honeymoon in Hawaii. She loved our little vacation spot so much that she's been dying to go back. In fact, I'm pretty sure she wouldn't have a problem with staying there forever to become a professional beach bum. I have to admit, the sun, sand, and ocean are a hell of a lot better than the windy city of Chicago.

I pull the car up to my parents' house and grab her bag out of the back. Preston has already arrived and he comes walking out.

"Hey, you guys got a minute?"

"Sure, what's up?" Piper asks as I set down our bags and close the trunk.

"Would it be cool if I brought a date to your wedding tomorrow?"

Piper laughs. "Really? Who?"

Preston looks at his feet as he kicks at the rocks. "Riley?"

"Riley? My maid of honor, Riley? She'll already be there," she points out. Then it hits her. "Wait, the two of you have been seeing each other?"

He wrinkles his nose like he's afraid to admit it. "Yeah . . . I mean, it's nothing serious, but after that dinner at your place, we kind of hit it off and have been hanging out here and there."

"That was three months ago, Preston. Why didn't you tell me?" She's obviously getting slightly annoyed, so I put my arm around her to calm her down.

"We just didn't want to tell you until we knew what we were doing. We didn't want our relationship to end badly and put a strain on you guys." He looks up at the sky for a moment. "Sounds familiar, doesn't it?"

I laugh and she rolls her eyes. "Preston, she's my best friend. I swear, if you treat her like the rest of your whores, this won't end well for us. Why would you risk our friendship like this?"

He frowns as he crosses his arms and leans against Dad's truck. "You mean like you risked our friendship by dating my brother?"

I don't say anything, I just wait. She shakes her head. "That was different. Calvin and I didn't blow through the opposite sex the way you do. What we had from the beginning was real, unlike anything you've ever had in your life."

I lean in and whisper in her ear. "I think you're overreacting, Piper."

She nods and takes a deep breath. "You're right. I'm sorry, Pres. It's just all the stress and the hormones."

"So, you're cool with Riley and me?"

She laughs and nods her head. "Well, I guess you found a way to sleep with the godmother after all, didn't you?"

Preston just shrugs and smiles.

"I need a nap," Piper says.

"Let's get you home." I lead her across the street to her parents' house. I carry her bag to her room then turn to give her a kiss. "I'll see you at the church." I press my lips against hers.

"I'll be the one in white," she whispers against my lips.

I kiss her for a while longer before pulling away. "Rest up, baby. You're going to need it." I flash her a grin before retreating.

Later that night, Preston, our dad, and I are sitting around the kitchen table with a glass of scotch. "Come on, Cal. You wouldn't let me throw you a bachelor party. At least celebrate your last night of being single."

I groan. "Fine, but I better not be hung over tomorrow," I point out.

Dad looks at me. "Well, we could always go across the street for some garage fun. No hangovers with that stuff."

I laugh. "No way. I'm never smoking again."

Preston laughs as he talks about all the stupid shit I said and did that day. I just hold up my middle finger.

Mom walks in with a photo album and sits with us. "While you're getting drunk, I thought it would be fun to take a walk down memory lane." She sets the book on the table and opens it up. The first picture is of her and my dad when they first got married. She turns the page and there's a picture of me right after I was born. Then Preston shows up on the scene. The following photos have us growing up and turning from babies to toddlers to kids. That's when Piper makes her way into the photos.

There's one of us climbing the tree in our backyard. In another, we're all sitting on the edge of the pool with our feet dangling in the water. We're all wearing arm floaties and eating Popsicles. There's Preston, Piper, and me. In fact, over the course of the rest of the book, it's pretty much the same—Piper right between my brother and me. It makes me laugh because she said she didn't want to be stuck between us forever, yet that's where she's always been.

The photos go through their teenage years, but I'm rarely in them. Most of the pictures are just of Preston and Piper. It almost makes me a little jealous, but then I realize that most of the photos from here on out will be of Piper and me. He got her for the first part of our lives, but for this part—the part that really matters—she's all mine. We're getting married, having a baby, and soon, I'll be right here doing this same thing with my child the night before his or her wedding. I smile, knowing that I wouldn't want it any other way.

———

I'M GETTING ready in the church with Preston—as well as Piper's brother, Jake—when my brother looks up at me. He's posing in front of a mirror. "Hey, Cal? You think Pipes would have a meltdown if I walked down the aisle wearing my Chucks instead of those uncomfortable dress shoes that came with the tux?"

I chuckle. "I think she'd stop the wedding and make everyone wait while you went to change."

Jake pipes up. "Yeah, don't do that. Let's not delay the boring part any longer than we have to. The reception is where it's at!" He smiles wide, and when he does, I see so much of Piper in him it isn't funny.

I haven't seen Jake in years. He's older than me and went off to college before I was even in high school. After college, I think he spent a summer at home before moving to the city, where he started working in insurance. He met his wife and they started a family, only recently moving from Chicago to New York for his work.

He helps straighten my tie. I'm so nervous that my hands are shaking. "Who knew that my kid sister would marry the kid across the street?" he says, looking at me fondly.

I laugh. "Yeah, let's just hope she doesn't run away with the other kid from across the street," I reply loudly enough for Preston to hear.

He turns around. "You know I'd never let her do that, right?"

I grunt, not sure of anything when it comes to those two.

"Seriously, she wouldn't even consider it. The two of you are so perfect together that I can't believe I didn't see it before. Plus, you've knocked her up. She ain't going nowhere, man," he laughs out, then stops as he realizes he's spilled the beans to her brother.

I look over at Jake and Jake looks at me. He smiles and raises his hands in the air, showing me his palms. "I didn't hear anything."

"Thanks. We're telling everyone at the reception, so you don't have to keep the secret for too long. Hell, I'm surprised my dumbass brother has kept it in until now." I glare at him and he shrugs.

"Sorry, man. It just slipped out."

"Mm-hmm, as long as it doesn't slip out again."

We get the knock on the door that indicates it's time to get this show on the road. The three of us walk out of the room and head to the chapel. We enter through the side door and take our places on the stage. The pews are already full of our friends and family, with our parents right up front—all but her dad, who's giving her away.

The preacher comes out and stands beside me. Moments later, the music starts up and the doors at the end of the aisle open. I stand there, watching as the flower girls walk out, dropping flower petals. Then Riley comes in with a smile. I look back at Preston and he's smiling at her too—and checking her out in her light-blue brides-maid's dress.

The music changes and gets louder. I see Piper step up to the door and she steals my breath. Her dad is at her side and I see his lips move, but can't hear what he's saying. He's probably trying to make sure she isn't backing out. Or maybe he's trying to talk her *into* backing out. I'm not sure.

Her honey-blonde hair is pulled up high on her head with soft curls falling around her face. Her white dress is long and beautiful, sparkling where the light hits it. It hugs her hips nicely and puts her growing breasts on display. I have to wet my dry lips and talk myself down before I do something to screw up the wedding—like fucking her right here on this stage in front of all our friends and family. I'm so lost in her that I don't even realize that the preacher has started talking.

THE WRONG BROTHER   183

"Who gives this woman to be married to this man?" I manage to hear over my thoughts.

"Her mother and I do," her father says, handing her over to me.

"You look beautiful," I whisper, and she smiles and mouths the words *thank you*.

The preacher starts talking about two people coming together as one, and I think there's a prayer in there somewhere, but I can't tear my eyes off her long enough to listen to what he's saying. All I know is that when I'm asked to repeat after him, I do so without even having to try. It's like I already know what I need to do. Like I've been prepared to say these words to her my whole life.

"I take you, Piper Lynn Montgomery, to be my wife, to have and to hold from this day forward. For better, for worse, for richer, for poorer, in sickness and in health, to love and to cherish, till death do us part." I slide the silver wedding band onto her finger and she smiles.

"I take you, Calvin Michael Young, to be my husband, to have and to hold from this day forward. For better, for worse, for richer, for poorer, in sickness and in health, to love and to cherish, till death do us part." She slides the matching silver wedding band onto my finger as we turn to look at the preacher.

"By the power vested in me by the state of Illinois, I now pronounce you husband and wife. You may kiss the bride."

Nothing else needs to be said. I pull her against me and press my mouth to hers. My tongue comes out and dances with hers and it feels like the first time. Everyone in the church cheers and claps. Preston clears his throat from behind me and it reminds me to pull away at some point.

Forcing myself, I pull back and her face is flushed. We turn toward the crowd and I lead her down the aisle. Once we're no longer in the chapel, we go into her private dressing room. The moment the door closes, I spin her around and press my body to hers, kissing her deeply. We're supposed to be waiting for everyone to go outside so they can throw birdseed at us, and I know the perfect way to kill a few minutes.

My hands start pushing her dress up her thighs.

She giggles against my lips. "What are you doing? We can't have sex in a church."

"Oh, but we can," I say, moving my hands to my pants to unfasten them. I push them down my thighs and push up her dress. When the dress is bunched up around her waist, I pick her up again and position myself at her opening.

She no longer cares where we are. I can tell by the way her mouth is back on mine as I guide myself into her. She moans into my mouth when we connect, and I'm already so excited I could come without even moving. But we only have a few minutes and I want to make sure she gets what she needs. I move my hips back and forth as fast as I can, pounding into her with everything I have. It only takes a couple minutes before she's shattering around me. When her muscles start to loosen, I finish myself off with a growl.

Someone knocks on the door. "All right guys, everyone is waiting for you," Preston says, and I'm glad it's him and not the church director or something.

With a sigh, I pull out of her and set her gently on her feet. I pull my pants up and help her get her dress and everything situated again. After I fasten my pants, I hold out my arm. "Ready for this, Mrs. Young?"

She smiles wide. "I like the sound of that." She laces her arm through mine and I open the door, leading her out of the church and onto the sidewalk where our friends and family are lined up, pelting us with birdseed. The limo is at the bottom of the steps and we rush to it, jumping inside and closing the door behind us.

Everyone outside the limo is still throwing birdseed and blowing bubbles, cheering and clapping as I pop open a bottle of sparkling cider. It bubbles as I pour it into a flute.

"Calvin, I can't." She seems surprised that I've forgotten she's pregnant and would even think of offering her alcohol.

I laugh and show her the bottle. "It's safe; I promise." I tap my glass against hers. "I'd never do anything to hurt you or our baby." I lean forward, press a kiss to her lips, then we each take a sip.

"Are you ready to tell our families the good news?" I ask as we drive around, waiting for everyone to get to the country club where we can be announced.

"I'm nervous," she confesses. "I just feel like everyone's going to judge us for moving so fast."

"We did move kind of fast," I agree. "But why wait when you know what you want?"

She offers up a soft smile. "I don't know how you do it, but you always know just what to say, exactly when I need to hear it."

"That's what I'm here for." I lean in and kiss her softly. My hand gently presses against her belly. "And soon, everyone is going to know about this little guy."

———

WE WALK into the country club and head toward the grand room. The DJ announces us and the doors open.

"Everyone, please give a warm welcome to Mr. and Mrs. Calvin Young!"

Everyone stands from their seats to clap and cheer for us as we enter the room that's been decorated perfectly. Every table has a white tablecloth with light-blue lace draped over it. In the center of each table sits a large jar holding a single tall candle, surrounded by baby's breath and little blue flowers.

We pose for pictures and are given handshakes and hugs on the way over to our table. Our chairs are in the center with Jake, Preston, and Riley close by. I can't tell how much time is spent just talking to everyone who comes up to our table, but after what feels like forever, it's time to cut the cake.

The moment of truth.

Piper makes sure our parents are front and center for the cake cutting. She picks up the knife and I place my hand on top of hers. We cut through it together and pull out a slice of cake. The icing is white with tiny blue flowers along the side. The cake itself is blue. Now, sure, our wedding colors are blue and white, so people probably just think we went overboard with the colors. But we place the slice on a plate and look up at our parents. Our fathers are completely lost. My mom seems confused—like she's trying to figure out why in the world we'd have a blue wedding cake. But Piper's mom lets out a loud squeal and tears flood her eyes.

"Oh my God! They're pregnant!" she announces loudly to the whole wedding party.

Our parents look to us for confirmation as we nod.

The room erupts in another round of applause as our parents come over to hug us. Preston is standing at my side and my mom looks at him. "Did you know about this?" There hasn't been much in our lives that the other hasn't known about.

He offers up a crooked smile. "I might have."

She looks back at me. "How in the world did you get this one to keep that big of a secret? How long have you known?" she asks, looking back at him.

"Since they got back from Hawaii."

She turns and looks back up at me, then over to Piper. "You're that far along?"

Piper smiles and nods.

"I can't believe you two!"

Piper's mom comes over to tell her about all the things she's knitted, and her dad seems to finally relax.

"What's wrong, Mr. M?" I ask around a smile.

He shakes his head and wipes the sweat off his brow. "I'm just glad that it's you two having the baby and not us! She really had me worried," he laughs out.

The party gets started and everyone is eating, drinking, dancing, and having a good time. I notice that Preston and Riley run off together, and it has me wondering if things are more serious with them than what they've been claiming. I don't bring it up to Piper, though. I want her to remember tonight as the night we finally made it official—not the night my brother hooked up with her best female friend.

We laugh and dance and do all the normal wedding things. I throw her garter and Preston makes sure to catch it just because he wants to win everything. He doesn't realize that if you catch the garter, it means you're getting married next. He even pushed people out of the way to catch it. Poor Uncle Wilbur nearly broke a hip.

After Preston helps pick him up off the floor and Uncle Wilbur ambles off, Preston holds the blue garter in the air in his closed fist. I walk over with a laugh. "You realize that means you're getting married next, right?"

His expression changes from happiness to worry in a split second. "What? No! No, it doesn't mean that! Does it? Here, you take it!"

I hold up my hands. "Sorry, I'm already married. That's all yours. And just think, that was probably Uncle Wilbur's last chance too."

"Uncle Wilbur!" he says, quickly looking around him in all directions. He finally finds him sitting at a table up front. Preston runs over, falls to his knees, and shoves the garter into his hand. Uncle Wilbur tries giving it back, but Preston is up and gone before that can happen.

Piper stands to throw the bouquet, and to everyone's surprise, my mom catches it. She's beyond happy, because she's been trying to talk my dad into renewing their vows for years now.

"It's perfect timing. Next year will be our 30th anniversary!"

Dad rubs his eyes and shakes his head.

I laugh as I walk away from them to find my bride. She's back at our table, sitting all alone. I take my seat next to her. "Everything okay?"

She nods and offers up a smile. "I'm just tired and my back is starting to hurt from being on my feet all day."

I take her hand in mine. "Well, let's get out of here then. Our honeymoon awaits."

"We can't leave our own party early."

"Who says we can't?" I ask, pulling her up to her feet and sneaking out the side door, not stopping to say any goodbyes.

I call Preston and he comes outside with Riley. "Riley is riding with me to keep me company on the way home. You guys got everything?" he asks, walking to his car in the parking lot.

"Yep, we have everything. I just need to change out of my dress before the flight. I'll do it in the back seat." Piper digs her clothes out of the bag and brings them into the back seat with us. As Preston drives us toward the airport, Piper strips out of her dress and stuffs it into the front seat for Riley to deal with.

Once she's fully changed, she leans in and presses a kiss to my lips. "I love you, Mr. Young."

I smile. "I love you too, Mrs. Young."

EPILOGUE
PIPER

"Careful, don't shake him too much," I say, watching Calvin as he carries Mason's car seat.

"I know. He's fine," Calvin says, setting the seat down in front of me. He bends down, unfastens him, and hands him over to me to breastfeed. I hold my little boy in my arms and gaze down at his handsome little face. He's the perfect mix of Calvin and me. He has Calvin's icy blue eyes and angular face, but the rest of him is all me. His honey-blond hair is all over the place from wiggling his way out of his little hat.

I lower my top and he latches on.

Calvin laughs. "He must get his appetite from his mama."

"Speaking of, I'm starving. Would you mind finding me something?"

"Sure." He stands up and moves into the kitchen. A little while later, he's bringing me a plate. He sets it on the arm of the couch while I burp Mason. I look over to find my favorite banana nut muffin from the bakery back home.

My eyes widen with excitement. "How'd you get that?"

He grins. "I have my ways." He collapses next to me on the

couch. "When Preston went home last week, I had him pick up a dozen. I froze them, so now you can have one whenever you want."

Tears fill my eyes. My hormones are still clearly screwed up. "You did that for me?"

He chuckles and nods his head. "Of course. I'd do anything for you, baby." He picks up my hand and kisses the back.

Someone knocks on the door and Preston and Riley walk in. They're still hiding their relationship from everyone, but I can tell things are getting more and more serious. We caught them out on an actual date a few days before I went into the hospital. I was desperate to get this baby out of me and had taken to walking him out. Calvin and I were on a stroll in the city when we bumped into them. They both blew it off and acted like it was nothing out of the ordinary, but we knew the truth.

"Hey, guys," Riley says as she comes to sit down. "We thought the godmother and godfather should meet the baby we've sworn to protect."

"Lucky you, he's just eaten."

"Yeah, he's like his mommy when it comes to food," Calvin jokes.

I roll my eyes at him and lean forward, passing Mason over to Riley.

She holds him close to her chest and gazes down at him like he's stolen her heart. "He's perfect," she cries out, tears starting to run down her cheeks.

"Aww, you okay, Riley?" I ask, grabbing a tissue off the end table and passing it over to her.

She takes it and wipes at her tears as she nods.

Preston is still standing up and looking nervous. "I'm just going to say it," he blurts out, stealing everyone's attention.

"What's up, man?" Calvin asks, suddenly looking nervous himself.

Preston takes a deep breath, puts his hands on his hips, and says, "Riley and I are pregnant!"

They both sit stock-still, watching us and waiting for our reaction.

Calvin's stuck in overly-friendly, smiley mode. "That's . . . great?" he says, but it sounds more like a question.

"You're pregnant?" I ask, looking only at Riley.

She nods, tears still falling from her eyes.

"Are you happy about this? Were the two of you planning this?"

"It wasn't planned, but we're happy. I know we haven't really known each other for very long, but since you introduced us, we haven't been able to leave each other's sides. After that dinner where you asked me to be godmother, we started talking and hanging out. Then we finally went out on a few dates, but we were taking it slow. I mean, I knew that you were in love with Calvin, but I still didn't know how you'd feel about me being with Preston since you'd loved him all of your life and he was your best male friend. In fact, we took things so slowly that we didn't hook up until your wedding."

"You hooked up for the first time at our wedding?" I ask, feeling excited. What could be better than my two best friends getting together? And they're having a baby! I'm going to be an aunt!

"This is perfect, guys," I finally say after processing my emotions. I stand up slowly and give Preston a hug. I can't hug Riley because she's holding Mason, but I promise to get her later.

We all sit and talk about Preston, Riley, and the new baby she's carrying. Then it hits me.

"We can finally buy our houses and live next door to each other!" I nearly yell, making Mason—who's now in Calvin's arms—jump.

Everyone laughs. "This place is almost done being renovated. It's the perfect time to put it on the market. We need to start looking for houses closer to home."

Everyone laughs and jokes about it, but I'm completely serious and already planning on checking out real estate websites tomorrow. As I sit back and watch my husband with our new baby, and my best friend with my other best friend, I know I have it all. There's nothing in life I can't handle, because now I know I already have everything I need.

HOW TO MARRY YOUR BEST FRIEND'S BFF SNEAK PEEK!

Read the romantic, swoon-worthy story of how Preston and Riley fall in love and get their happily ever after in *How to Marry Your Best Friend's BFF*

CHAPTER 1

PRESTON

Pregnant. My best friend, the one who—up until a few months ago—was in love with me, is now pregnant and marrying my brother. How the fuck did we get here? I feel like my whole world is a snow globe and someone just grabbed it off it's perfect little shelf and shook the ever loving shit out of it. My best friend who has always been by my side was picked up and thrown across the globe, landing in my brother's arms. I know one thing for sure, this is a summer I'll never forget.

I think back to that Fourth of July weekend we spent at home—the one where I told Piper that I was in love with her.

"I think I might be in love with you, Piper."

She giggles. "I don't think so, Preston. I think you're just confused about seeing me and Calvin together so much. Maybe even a little jealous?" She looks up at me from beneath her long, dark lashes and bites down on her bottom lip. It only makes me remember how soft they were against mine, how sweet.

"Maybe, but here lately, I look at you and see how beautiful you are and how much you've grown up. Maybe it's time for me to grow up

too. If I could do that, then we could be together because then I wouldn't ruin this."

My words must scare her because she stands up and takes a step back, like she doesn't even know who I am anymore and she doesn't want to be this close to a stranger. "No, Preston. We can never be together. You were right. We're friends. We'll always be friends, but we couldn't ever be more. I love you. I do. You're my best friend and I'd do anything in the world for you, but I'm not in love with you. In fact, I don't think I was in love with you when I took you on that show. I just thought I was."

I stand up and move toward her. "Are you saying that if I kissed you right now, you'd push me away?"

She licks her lips like she's preparing for our kiss, but she nods her head. "Yes. Pres, we can't go there. If you were thinking straight, you'd see that, just like you did before. Don't let my friendship with Calvin confuse you into thinking you want something you don't."

I take another step. "You'd push me away?" I can't help the smirk that forms. "Let's find out." I take one more step forward, reach for her, and pull her against my chest, my lips finding hers. Fuck, her lips are just as soft as I remember them being. So damn sweet and teasing. Her body seems to mold to mine as her scent travels up my nose and intoxicates me. What the fuck was I thinking before? How could I not want this every day? She's perfect for me. She's always been perfect. She's always had my back, even when I was in the wrong. That's how much she believe's in me. I was selfish for keeping her on the hook the way I did. I was just too afraid of screwing up and losing her for good.

I move my lips against hers, but she doesn't budge. She doesn't kiss back. As a last resort to make her see, I slide my tongue into her mouth. It only brushes against her's for a moment before she's pushing me away. "See, there's nothing between us. Did you feel tingles? See fireworks? Did that kiss make your heart race, your breathing pick up?"

Yes.

She shakes her head. "It didn't mine. I think you should go, Preston."

I really made a mess of things that night. She was right about one thing. I was confused by her and Calvin's closeness. But she was also wrong. I am in love with her. But I'm a dumb ass for not realizing it sooner. I love her enough to let her go and be happy. That's what she deserves after all.

I think I've been doing a good job at keeping my feelings hidden. I really am happy for the both of them. Calvin told me how he's always had a thing for her. Looking back now, I don't know how I didn't see it before. And Piper deserves someone like Calvin who will love her whole heartedly, take care of her, and be there when she needs. There's no way I'm going to screw up what the two of them have finally found.

But that also leaves me feeling a little alone. Before, I had two people to fall back on when I was bored or lonely. Now, those two people are together and when I'm around, I feel like I'm butting into their personal moment. I think the only chance I have at getting over Piper will be to find someone for myself.

Find someone who I could love and someone who could love me back. I mean, I'm twenty-five years old and I've never in my life been in a serious relationship before. At the time of the show, I couldn't see myself with Piper or anyone for that matter. All I wanted to do was have fun. Go out drinking. Take trips and adventures. I didn't want anyone holding me back from living my life the way I wanted. But now that Calvin and Piper are set to get married and they're having a baby, it makes me see how stupid I've been. I wouldn't be trading in one life for another. I would be creating more life, more to love, more moments to share with someone special.

It's settled. I will force myself to grow up, to find someone I want to spend my life with. Being single is great and fun, but being alone sucks. Now that I've decided that I want to be in a relationship, where do I go to find one? That's something I've always avoided before. It's not like I can just run on down to Target and be like, uh, yes I would like one girlfriend, please? I can't get online and order one from Amazon either. How do people meet people?

Ugh, I'm not even in a relationship yet and it's already driving me crazy.

Either way, I don't have time to think about it because I'm crashing some kind of dinner that Calvin and Piper have planned. I wasn't exactly invited, but I heard them talking about it and her friend Riley. I figured if she's going to be acting the part of godmother, I needed to be involved too.

I pull on my shoes and leave my apartment, climbing behind the wheel and making the drive over to her house. There's a strange car in the drive when I pull up and can only assume it belongs to Riley. I smile to myself as I climb out and help myself into the house, and into the fridge where I grab two beers. I slip one into my pocket and open the other, taking a drink as I step out onto the patio. The three of them are already all on the patio, surrounding the grill.

I look her up and down. "Who's this?"

Piper rolls her eyes at my bluntness. "Preston, this is Riley. Riley, Preston. He's Calvin's brother and my best friend since kindergarten."

Riley looks up to me and this funny thing happens. I forget to breathe. I've never seen anyone like her. She's beautiful with her sun kissed skin and chocolatey eyes. When the wind blows, a tree branch moves and allows the sunlight to hit her perfectly. Those chocolate eyes also have a hint of caramel to them. Her long, sleek black hair blows in the wind behind her like she's in a damn shampoo commercial. I feel myself inhale trying to get a scent of her shampoo. *Did I just sniff the air like a damn dog?*

She holds out her hand to shake. "It's nice to finally meet the man who broke my best friend's heart on national television."

My mouth opens but I don't know what the fuck to say to that shit. She's straight up calling me out. I look from her, to Piper, and then Cal. "Ummmm, I..." Yep, nothing. Still can't think of anything to say.

She busts out laughing, showing me her perfectly, straight, white teeth. Yup, she's perfect. "I'm just messing with ya. Relax."

I feel the anxiety leave me in a wave, but have to sit down. I didn't realize that I'd been holding my breath and now I'm feeling a little light headed.

Everyone takes a seat and Calvin reaches over to hold Piper's hand. "Riley, we actually have something to tell you," she starts.

"Wow, I feel like this is very formal. And all without a drink in my hand."

I pull the beer out of my pocket and hand it over. It's the least I can do.

She laughs. "Thanks." She pops it open and takes a sip, turning her attention back to Piper and my brother.

Piper swallows down her nervousness. "As you know, Calvin and I are getting married this winter."

Riley nods.

"Well, the reason we're having the wedding so soon is because I'm pregnant!"

Riley's eyes bug out and her mouth drops open, the corners turning up slightly. "What? Seriously?"

Piper smiles and nods. "And since me and you are so close, I was wondering if you would consider being the baby's godmother."

"Godmother? That's a thing?" she asks, pulling her brows together as she picks at the label on the bottle.

"I mean, it's mostly just a promise to help guide the baby when he needs it. Be a parent to it if Calving and I ever die in a fiery crash or something," Piper tells her.

"Uh okay wow that went dark. Wait, who's the godfather?" she asks.

You rang?

I smile wide and holds up my hand. "It's going to be me and you, baby." I wink at her, almost blowing her a kiss but I hold back.

"That in no way, shape, or form means that you two get to have sex," Piper says pointing a finger between the two of us, killing all the fun. She used to be fun, but when she got with my brother, that all went out the window.

"I'm sorry what?" she asks.

Piper waves off her question. "Preston is stupid and thought that him being the godfather was a free pass to try out the godmother."

"I'm still down to try too," I offer, wagging my brows and nodding my head.

"Riley, I'm sorry my brother is such a dumb ass," Calvin says, glaring at me. He's clearly afraid that I'm going to chase her off.

Riley laughs. "Yes, I'll do it."

"You will?" Piper asks.

She nods. "Yes, how can I pass up being a member of this family?"

Piper stands up and pulls her in for a hug. "Thank you so much. And don't worry about Preston. We all just beat the shit out of him when he needs it. Now that you're in the family, you have that right too." Piper smiles over at me.

"Hey!" I blurt out.

Piper rolls her eyes but they pull apart and take their seats once again. "Now that that's done," She looks over at Riley. "I'll get you your wine. Preston, I guess you'll need another beer since you gave Riley your spare?"

I shoot her a grin. "You know it."

She shakes her head but stands up to move into the kitchen.

Calvin flips the steaks and goes inside, saying something about a water bottle.

I look over and find Riley still picking at the label on her bottle. "So, you're Riley?"

She glances over at me and nods while forcing a smile. "And you're the famous Preston I've heard so much about."

I smile. "I'm famous?"

She shrugs one shoulder. "Mostly as the asshole who ran away from a beautiful woman on TV, so more like infamous. What is wrong with you?" she asks around a laugh.

I let out a sigh and rub my hand over my face. "I don't even know anymore," I admit, and it's true. Not a day passes that I don't wish I could go back and relive that day, tell Piper that I love her too. Then maybe my little snow globe would be reset.

She reaches over and places her hand on my arm. "Hey, we all make mistakes. It's just not usually on national TV." She offers up a breathtaking smile and I can't help but to laugh with her.

I shake my head. "I'm never going to live that down, am I?"

She purses her lips together and seems to mull it over. "Maybe. Maybe not. I guess we'll just have to see."

I know nothing about Riley, but already I can tell she's as big of a flirt as I am. So naturally, I'm drawn to her like a moth to the flame.

Calvin comes back out and sprays down the flames on the grill. I pay him no mind as I take in Riley. She's completely oblivious to the fact that I'm staring at her and I like that about her. I can tell she's the no-bullshit type of girl. She doesn't think the world owes her something because of her looks. Fuck, I bet she doesn't even know how beautiful she is. I love her style too. She's wearing a short pair of cut-off jean shorts that are light in color like they've been acid washed. They show off her long, tanned legs perfectly. Her glossy black toenails pop against her Birkenstock sandals. Her shirt has The Stroke's album cover on it, but the sleeves and the bottom of the shirt have been cut off, reveling her beautiful shoulders and tight abdomen. I can't help but to lick my lips as I take her in. She's effortlessly cool, like she gave no thought to the kick ass outfit she put together, yet she pulls it off seamlessly.

"Preston, can I talk to you for a minute?" Calvin asks, nearly making me jump.

"Uh, yeah. Sure." I stand and walk with him into the kitchen just as Piper is walking back out with a glass of wine for Riley and a bottle of beer for me. She hands off the beer before slipping out the sliding glass door.

I finish off my beer and toss the bottle into the trash can before opening the new one. "What's up, man?"

He turns to face me and his face is red. I wonder what he's angry about. "I'm only going to say this once so pay attention. Okay?"

I nod and take another drink.

"Riley is off limits. Got that? No friendship between you two. No dates. No hook-up's. No relationship of any kind. Okay?"

"Of course," I say putting my hands up like I have no idea what he's talking about. "I don't even know the girl. Damn, what crawled up your ass and died?" I lean against the island in the center of the kitchen.

"I know you don't know her, but I saw the way you were looking at her out there. There's drool all over your shirt right now. And you're Preston."

I look down at it but there isn't. What's he talking about? "No there's not," I argue.

He hangs his head and lets out a long breath. "Just repeat after me, I will not have any contact with Riley."

I roll my eyes. "What's the big deal?"

"The big deal?" His eyes widen. "The big deal is that she's my fiancé's best friend. I know how you are. You'll reel her in, take what you want, then leave her hurt and broken hearted. She'll come crying to Piper, then Piper will be upset. And she doesn't need that stress with the baby. So, I want you to repeat after me... I will not have any contact with Riley."

"I will not have any contact with Riley, yeah yeah. I get it. Happy now?"

He smiles and nods his head. "Very. Now, let's go back outside. We don't want to be rude." He grabs a tray of food and heads back out onto the patio. I stand back and watch him go, annoyed that he took away my best friend but is now telling me who I can and can't date? Who does he think he is? Obviously anything that happens between us will stay between us and as long as I'm upfront about my intentions, what's the problem?

What are my intentions? I just told myself to stop with the random hook-up's and try to find someone I want to spend the rest of my life with. Could that be Riley? Who knows but I won't find out till I get a taste. I really should get to know her better before I decide. I grab my beer and go back out, taking my seat.

"So, Riley, you work with Piper at the magazine?" I ask.

Her dark eyes find mine and she smiles a little before nodding. "Yeah, that's right. We met in college and became good friends right off the bat. It was completely by chance that we ended up at the same place, but I'm glad we did. It's fun working with your best friend."

I look over at Calvin and it looks like he's shooting daggers at me with his eyes, but I ignore him and turn my attention back to her. "You guys both write the same kind of pieces?"

"It's really just luck of the draw. No two pieces are the same and you just get what you get." She shrugs. "What is it that you do, Preston?"

"I'm one of the systems analyst for the Chicago Cubs. I can get you into any game you want." I flash her a smile.

"That's impressive," she replies. "I love baseball so I might take you up on that."

"Any time."

"Riley, have I shown you the room we're going to be using for the baby?" Piper jumps in to ask.

"No, not yet."

"Come on. I'll show you and you can help me decide on a color." The two of them get up and walk into the house, leaving me alone with Calvin.

"Do we need to repeat it again?" he asks.

I scoff. "No, man. I was just trying to be friendly. I mean, if we're going to be the godparents, figured we be thrown together a lot and I should play nice. That's all. You act like I can't even have a conversation with her without it suddenly turning into a porno."

"Mm-hmm," he mumbles as he sets down the tongs and comes to sit at the table.

The girls end up coming back outside but Piper keeps her and Riley's conversation so full that I don't even get a chance to talk again.

After the first fifteen minutes, I give up and resort to occupying myself with my drink. Dinner is finally ready and after that much steak, I'm ready to crash.

I push away from the table. "Well guys, thanks for dinner but I think I'm going to take off. Riley," I turn to face her. "It was nice to meet you."

She looks up at me with her big, brown eyes and smiles. "You too, Preston, but guys," she turns to face them. "I think I'm going to take off too. I have to work in the morning and I haven't even had a chance to get anything done around the house."

Calvin and Piper end up walking us both to the door and there's so much talking I don't even understand it. When the door closes, I let out a long breath. "Man, they sure can talk, can't they?"

Riley laughs and nods as we head down the front steps. "They sure can, but they're happy so it's understandable."

"Yeah, I guess you're right." We make it to the driveway and she stops at her car door. It feels like she's waiting for something else. "Hey, are you busy right now? Want to grab a coffee and hang out or something?"

She looks me up and down with her lips pressed tightly together. But they turn up slightly in the corners. "Yeah, I got a few minutes I guess."

I smile. "Meet me at the Starbucks on the corner across from Walgreens?"

"Sure." She gets into her car and I turn around to climb into mine.

A little while later, I'm pulling up to her already parked car. I climb out just as she does, meeting in the front of our vehicles. I open the door for her and we both walk in. With it being so late in the day, the place isn't busy so we place our order and move to the end of the counter to get our coffee. I notice that she drinks the same thing as Piper and that makes me smile as I take my coffee and move to sit at a table.

"So, what do you think about all this godparent business?" I ask, wanting to break the ice.

She laughs. "Oh, man. Do they even know who they asked?" she asks, eyes wide with confusion. "I mean, I've never held a kid in my life! And I'm not exactly the role model type if you know what I mean. I go on too many dates, drink entirely way too much, and can't force myself to be a normal adult. That shit sucks!"

I laugh. "God, I'm glad it's not just me. I know nothing about kids. I just hope this is more of a title than an actual job. We're supposed to help guide the kid? If he comes to me with a question, I'm sure I'll probably tell him the exact wrong thing to do. I mean, I can't even guide myself!"

She laughs and nods. "Same. It's so crazy that they're even having kids already. I don't mean because they haven't been together that long because they've known one another their whole lives. I just meant... she's twenty-five! That's how old I am and I couldn't imagine having a kid right now. I'm still a kid myself."

I let out a sigh. "Finally, someone understands me. I mean, it's not 1940 anymore. We have more choices now. We're not expected to get married and start popping out kids as soon as we're legal. I don't want to rush into things, you know. I just want to kick back, take it easy, and have fun. I couldn't imagine getting off work and coming home to a family."

"I agree one-hundred percent." She nods.

I pick up my coffee and take a sip, trying to think of something else to talk about. "So, you like The Strokes?" I ask, pointing to her T-shirt.

"Oh absolutely. What kind of music do you listen to?" She leans forward and so do I.

"I like everything honestly. I like alternative, rock, some rap. I like a lot of stuff I grew up on. My parents were always blasting 80's rock."

"Mine too."

The two of us sit at Starbucks until we're kicked out. We talk about music, movies, books, and sports. I feel like I'm actually getting to know her a little and it just leaves me wanting to know more. A part of me was hoping to get to know her so I'd find something that would draw me to her a little less with Calvin's warning, but that totally backfired on me. Everything I discovered just made me like her that much more.

I walk her out to her car and we're talking about that damn show that Piper took me on. She's laughing at my panicked expression and the way I ran off stage, ripping at the microphone. I can't help but to laugh with her. Not that I think it's funny, but I love the way she laughs so freely. I love the way that she's not always serious, that she knows how to kick back and have a little fun.

We stop at her driver's side door and she puts her hand on the handle but doesn't move to open it.

As our laughing dies down, I say, "Well, thanks for coming out with me. I had a really good time."

She nods and offers me a smile. "I did too. Now I know why Piper was always talking about you. You're a fun guy. We should do this again sometime."

I can't hold back my smile. "I'd like that," I say, feeling myself being pulled closer to her.

She looks up at me and wets her lips. Without overthinking, I lean in and press mine to hers. They're soft, so soft, and welcoming. Her tongue comes out and finds mine as her hands move up to my neck. Her fingers lace through my hair as she pulls me closer and deepens our little kiss. My body comes alive in ways that I've never experienced before. There's this wave of tingles that starts in my stomach and floods my body. My stomach tightens and flips. My heart races and my lungs work harder for air. I'm only just getting started when she breaks the kiss and takes a step back.

She smiles up at me. "Good night, Preston."

I return her smile. "Night, Riley." I step back and watch as she climbs into her car, backs up, and then drives away. I stand there, motionless until her taillights are no longer in view.

Calvin asked me to stay away and it seemed like Piper was on his side, yet I've never been good about listening. They both know that. I was told not to have contact with her and I kissed her. I should feel ashamed of myself, but I don't. I only feel happy and excited to see where this leads.

GRAB *How to Marry Your Best Friend's BFF HERE!*

READ THE REST OF THE LOVE YOU FOREVER SERIES HERE!

How to Marry Your Best Friend's BFF

Rocking His Fake World

How to Break-up with your Boss

ALSO BY ALEXIS WINTER

Slade Brothers Series

Billionaire's Unexpected Bride

Off Limits Daddy

Baby Secret

Loves Me NOT

Best Friend's Sister

Castille Hotel Series

Hate That I Love You

Business & Pleasure

Baby Mistake

Fake It

South Side Boys Series

Bad Boy Protector-Book 1

Fake Boyfriend-Book 2

Brother-in-law's Baby-Book 3

Bad Boy's Baby-Book 4

Mountain Ridge Series

Just Friends: Mountain Ridge Book 1

Protect Me: Mountain Ridge Book 2

Baby Shock: Mountain Ridge Book 3

Make Her Mine Series

My Best Friend's Brother

Billionaire With Benefits

My Boss's Sister

My Best Friend's Ex

Best Friend's Baby

ALL BOOKS CAN BE READ AS STAND-ALONE READS WITHIN THESE SERIES

ABOUT THE AUTHOR

Alexis Winter is a contemporary romance author who loves to share her steamy stories with the world. She specializes in billionaires, bad boys, alpha males and the women they love.

If you love to curl up with a good romance book you will certainly enjoy her work. Whether it's a story about an innocent young woman learning about the world or a sassy and fierce heroin who knows what she wants you,'re sure to enjoy the happily ever afters she provides.

When Alexis isn't writing away furiously, you can find her exploring the Rocky Mountains, traveling, enjoying a glass of wine or petting a cat.

You can find her books on Amazon or here: https://www. alexiswinterauthor.com/

Printed in Great Britain
by Amazon